CRYSTAL NOTICED SOMEONE OUT IN THE ENTRY-way, sorting through the coats. She recognized Shawn's profile and started to call to him. But she shut her mouth when she saw him stuff something in a coat pocket, then walk away. She hurried to the coats and picked hers up. She searched both pockets, but found nothing. As she laid it down, she brushed against Gabrielle's coat, feeling something in her pocket. She looked up to see if anyone was watching, then pulled a little, square box out of the pocket.

"A present? From Shawn to Gabrielle? Is he—?" Suddenly Crystal felt very, very sick.

Josh M.

CRYSTAL'S BLIZZARD TREK

STEPHEN AND JANET BLY

Chariot Books
DAVID C. COOK PUBLISHING CO.

A Quick Fox Book

Published by Chariot Books,
an imprint of David C. Cook Publishing Co.

David C. Cook Publishing Co., Elgin, Illinois 60120
David C. Cook Publishing Co., Weston, Ontario

CRYSTAL'S BLIZZARD TREK
© 1986 by Stephen and Janet Bly

Cover illustration by Paul Turnbaugh
Cover and book design by Chris Patchel

First Printing, 1986
Printed in the United States of America
90 89 88 87 86   1 2 3 4 5

Library of Congress Cataloging-in-Publication Data

Bly, Stephen A.
  Crystal's blizzard trek.

  (A Quick fox book)
  Summary: Rivals on a high school rodeo team learn to
come to terms with each other when they become trapped in
a blizzard in the Montana mountains.
  [1. Rodeos—Fiction. 2. Blizzards—Fiction. 3. Montana—
Fiction] I. Bly, Janet. II. Title.
PZ7.B6275Cm 1986   [Fic]   86-16721
ISBN 1-55513-055-0

For PAULA and CONDA
Lil' Sisters

CONTENTS

1
A NEW TECHNIQUE

THE MAIN DIFFERENCE BETWEEN SNOW AND rain: snow's a lot quieter. Anyway, that's the way it seemed to Crystal LuAnne Blake during her first winter in Winchester, Idaho.

"Look at this! Look at this, Karla." Crystal pulled back the front curtains of the Blake living room and pointed out to the yard. Six inches of new snow had fallen during the night. The front deck sidewalk was piled and rounded with fluffy waves, like miniature sand dunes blown across the desert.

"There's no way we're going to Montana to that rodeo next week," Crystal asserted as she clutched her furry, green bathrobe around her and tried to dry her wet hair. She bent over from the waist, letting her long, blonde hair drape over a heater vent.

Karla, her high school senior sister, looked blankly at her a moment, then kept digging in the entryway closet. "Crys . . . where's my blue sweater with the teddy bears?"

"Er . . . well, it's in the dirty clothes. I was attacked by a herd of pepperoni, and it was all I could do to escape with my life." Crystal kept rubbing her towel through her hair.

"What you mean is, you spilled pizza on my good sweater." Karla frowned. "Crystal, that's the last time . . ."

"Yeah, but Mom said she could get it out. Hey, do you want to hear something weird? Teresa Patterson eats pizza from the crust in. . . . You know, she doesn't start down at the point like everyone else, but she eats the crust, then the wide part. Wild, huh?"

Crystal stood up and walked to the window. "You know, I never heard it snow. I mean, you wake up and think nothing's happened all night, open up your curtains and, pow—there's all this white stuff everywhere. I like it that way—cold, clean, mysterious."

"Snow, mysterious?" Karla laughed and headed back up the stairs.

Mr. Blake came down from the upper level of the tri-level home and headed for the kitchen. Crystal sauntered into the kitchen and plopped down on a breakfast stool. "Dad, do you think they will cancel the trip to Kalispell?"

"Well, Christmas is the snow time of the year. They knew that before they scheduled this. I hear that the arena is really large, for an indoor one. I figure as long as they can get through Highway 12 to Missoula, the rest will be easy. Remember, everyone else is used to a snowy winter. We're the southern Californians," he smiled.

"Hey, did you hear me tell Mom? Megan said

10

in her letter that it was ninety-four back home. Ninety-four! Would you believe that?"

"Sure, I used to live there, remember?" Mr. Blake grinned as he fried some eggs.

"Boy, it seems like a long time ago. . . . You, me, and Megan driving into Kamiah. . . . Dad! I almost forgot, Megan said she could come up during Easter vacation. Mom said it was OK, I mean, is it OK?"

"Sure, but you'll be tied up with rodeo."

"Yeah, but I can't wait for her to meet everyone."

"She already knows Shawn." Mr. Blake raised his eyebrows with the touch of a tease in his eyes.

"Not to worry. Listen, Megan met this boy at school named Barron Brandorf. How's that for a name? Anyway, he's really cute and really rich. Sounds like the perfect guy for Megan.

"Dad, do you think the road's too icy to trailer Caleb over to Teresa's for some practice? We haven't done a whole lot of work since Pendleton, and we do want to have a good showing at Bitterroot Winter Rodeo in Kalispell."

"I'll tell you what, princess," he scooped up a couple eggs for Crystal. "Let me haul Caleb over to Pattersons' this morning. I've got to head across the prairie anyway. Then you go home with Teresa, and you'll be all set. I don't want you driving on this ice, not until you get that license, anyway."

"A week from Saturday. Can you believe it? If I pass my test I can have a driver's license by age fourteen and a half!"

"Oh, I believe it," Mr. Blake sighed. "I can hardly wait to see the insurance bill."

Crystal figured that the last three days of school before Christmas break would be fairly easy. Not one of the 106 students of Highland High felt like studying. Unfortunately, someone neglected to tell the teachers. By the end of the week she had a six-page report due in English, a speech scheduled in Drama I, and a big algebra test.

She sank into the chair in her first-period class and gazed over at her friend, Gabrielle Northstar. "You know, Gabrielle, school would be really great if it weren't for the classes we have to take. . . . Hey, that's a new sweater. It looks great. What color is that?"

"It's called Passionate Plum. What do you think?" she giggled.

"I think it makes you look . . . uh, a bit dangerous."

"Dangerous?"

"Yeah, if I see Shawn hanging around you very much, you're in real danger," Crystal explained.

"Well, it's a Christmas present from Uncle Sam," Gabrielle added. "Reservation Indians get a government check. Indian bribe money, I call it."

The whole subject of Indian life on the Nez Perce Reservation always bothered Crystal, so she changed the subject. "Hey, I'm going over to Teresa's for some practice. Are you coming?"

"Nah, I've got basketball practice. How are you and Teresa getting along?" Gabrielle opened her book and flipped through the pages.

"She's OK. Really! As long as we just talk horses, rodeo, and stuff. And she really is a good rider."

"Yeah, I can't argue that. I've never seen anyone, white or Indian, who wanted to win more than Teresa. Sometimes it's challenging to watch her, and sometimes it's just frightening. Know what I mean?" Gabrielle's voice trailed off as Teresa waltzed into the classroom and ceremoniously took her place on the other side of Crystal.

"Hey, Lil' Flash, you coming over to ride?" She spoke loud enough for the entire freshman class of nineteen students to hear.

"Yeah, Dad's bringing Caleb over this morning. Can I catch a ride home with you?"

"Sure, you can be one of the first to try out my Christmas present. A brand-new Ford Bronco. Red, of course."

"No kidding? It's all yours?"

"Well, it sort of belongs to the whole family, but I got to bring it to school. Tough, huh?"

"Yeah, it's mean, dirty work, but someone has to drive that new red Bronco," Crystal laughed.

13

"Are you giving your speech today?" Teresa asked.

"Not until Friday, how about you?"

"Tomorrow. I'm talking about how to raise thoroughbreds," Teresa nodded.

Crystal looked back over to Gabrielle who raised her eyebrows and sighed.

Teresa hadn't been kidding about the new Bronco. Crystal met her in the small parking lot in front of the gym. Several of the guys were admiring the new vehicle.

"Teresa, has your daddy got any more of these lying around?" one of the older fellows kidded.

"Yeah, Teresa, you want to go to the movies on Saturday? If you can't make it, that's OK, just send your Bronco," another hooted.

Eddie Valentine ran across the parking lot yelling, "At last! At last!" He ran right to the front of the Bronco and hugged the hood. Then he turned to the other guys and proclaimed, "At last—I'm in love!"

Teresa opened the door and stood up on the floorboard, looking over the crowd. "All right, peasants . . . back . . . back. . . . Eat your little, jealous hearts out." Crystal climbed in from the passenger side, and the two girls slid out of the parking lot, rocks flying and boys shouting.

"Isn't this great?" Teresa called as she pulled onto the state highway and headed through town and out into the country.

"My grandfather homesteaded here in the 1890s, when parts of the Indian reservation were opened up for public purchase," Teresa explained as they rode toward the ranch. "And Mom's family has silver mines in northern Idaho. I can't imagine living anywhere else in the world."

Crystal had been to the Pattersons' indoor arena dozens of times in the past several months. But she had never been to the Pattersons' house. Even in the winter snow the big, red-brick and wood-siding ranch house was impressive. A white rail fence surrounded the corrals and pastures next to the house. The stable was one of the plushest Crystal could imagine. She trailed Teresa into the house.

Crystal stood in amazement at the trophies and awards in the den. Both Teresa's mom and dad had spent years on the professional rodeo circuit.

"Are these your sisters?" Crystal gawked at a wall filled with pictures of girls riding at various rodeo events.

"Yeah, Tina is 28, Tracy 26, Trudy 24, Tammi 22, and Trisha is 20. Then, six years later, the one and only, Teresa."

"Wow! Six girls! I thought having three in the family was enough." Crystal plunged down into a huge leather chair. Teresa disappeared into the kitchen and reappeared with two soft drinks in hand.

"Oh, it's not too bad, being the youngest; it's like having five extra moms around. There was always someone to teach me to ride. I've followed them around to rodeos since the day I was born. Do you know that all five of them have been either State Rodeo Queen or State All Around Cowgirl?"

"No kidding? That's something!" Crystal stood back up and read some of the inscriptions on the trophies.

"Yeah, and Trudy was the National High School Rodeo Queen her senior year at Highland. Tammi's the best rider. She was in the National Finals down in Las Vegas earlier this month."

"Where are they all now? I mean, are any at home?" Crystal asked.

"Well, Tina is married and lives in Kellogg. She and David, her husband, look after the silver mines up there. David is a lawyer. Tracy and her husband are geologists with the government. They're down in Arizona doing some research on the Grand Canyon. Trudi is studying to be a veterinarian at the University of Idaho. She comes home a lot, but has a job in Moscow. I told you about Tammi, she's in and out depending on her travel schedule.

"And there's good old Trish. . . . She sort of runs the ranch. I mean she heads the haying, harvesting, calving, and elk hunting for the whole business. I guess she's trying hard to be

16

the son Dad never had."

"And then there's Teresa."

"Yeah, I'm the baby. Not too much required of me, just possess all the best qualities of the whole family." Teresa leaped up suddenly. "Let's get out to the arena."

The tone in Teresa's voice told Crystal there was more to the story, but she didn't press further. They rounded up their horses and saddled up.

"Hey," Teresa blurted, "you never told me about your family."

"Pretty dull. Karla gets all the pressure to be first, Allyson gets all the attention as baby, and I get to be left alone most of the time," Crystal replied. "It's sort of nice, really."

"Well, let's ride. After we warm these guys up, how about riding the poles?" Teresa called as she mounted her horse.

"Sure, I need to get better. I never can seem to do very well with them," Crystal shrugged.

It was Crystal's first time to ride in the arena without the whole rodeo team and coaches present. It seemed much larger and more awesome. The girls rode a circle around the arena, and, then Teresa turned in to a large figure eight pattern. Crystal followed.

She tried to imagine what it would be like to be Teresa and ride in that big, old arena day after day, all by herself. You could pretend to be in front of a great crowd, Crystal thought, and

17

give them your best ride, jump off your horse, and bow to the cheering fans. Crystal had a sudden urge to be in the arena all by herself and practice bowing to the crowds.

Instead, she climbed off her big, gray Appaloosa, and helped Teresa set up the poles. She never did understand why they called it pole bending, since there was no way those six-foot-tall, two-inch-thick poles would ever bend. It was more a slalom run. The rider raced to the far end of the long line of six poles, wove her way around them and back out again, and returned to the finish line.

The girls took turns running the course and timing each other. Teresa usually finished from three to five seconds ahead of Crystal. They stopped to give the horses a rest, dismounted, led their horses to the rail, and loosened the cinches. Both girls scrambled to the top of the fence and stared at the empty arena.

"Hey, you had really good times," Crystal began.

"Yeah, well, they are good enough for these little rodeos, but if I want to win at the state and national level, I need a couple more seconds off that time. I don't know if Hawkeye is the horse to do it. Maybe I need to buy a new horse."

"Another horse? But I thought you'd been riding this one a long time."

"Maybe that's the problem. I think I've pushed him about as fast as he can go," Teresa said as she studied her sorrel gelding.

"You're kidding, aren't you?" Crystal shook her head. "I mean, you don't just up and push aside a horse you've had a long time."

"Oh, come on, Crystal. It's not the horse that's important, it's winning. Look, if Caleb there hadn't turned out to be so good at cutting, you would have him up for sale by now. You'll never do a whole lot in poles or barrels with him," Teresa chided.

"Sell Caleb?" Crystal repeated, stunned. "I can't ever imagine doing that!"

"I've heard that before. Wait until you've gone to a state meet or two. Suddenly you'll do anything to be in contention. You'll get desperate enough even to sell your sister's diary. If you know what I mean," Teresa laughed. "Anyway, I can tell you how to lower your pole bending time even with Caleb."

Teresa reached down to the back of her boots and pointed. "These, to start with. You need to start wearing spurs. Oh, they can just be little ones with small, dull rowels, but if he can't feel a little side pain, he won't know to speed it up. Not only that, but you've got to use your quirt a lot more."

"My what?"

"Your whip. You've got to beat on him more if you're going to improve your time. I think most horses, like most people, are lazy. If you don't beat on them, they don't do their best."

"I just can't beat on him. . . . I mean, I really think Caleb is doing his best."

"Doing his best? He's just hanging back, loafing as far as I can see. Here, you wear my spurs, and slap his face with . . ."

"His face?"

"Yeah, that rump is so tough he wouldn't feel hardly anything. You slap his face, and I bet you can lower your time by closer to three seconds." Teresa started to pull off the spurs.

"I don't know, Teresa. I mean, Caleb and I are sort of a team. You know, he does his part and I do mine. I see us as kind of equal partners." "Well, that sounds dumb and naive, but you're new at it. Come on, just one ride and I guarantee that you'll have a better time. Look, if you're going to be a serious rider, then you'll want to push that gray to his limits. Go ahead, I'll time you."

"Just once," Crystal said uncertainly. "When do I spur him?"

"Kick him good as you begin, then spur him every turn just as you cross the center line of the poles. When you're making your last pass along the outside, really pour it on. And don't forget to slap his face a little."

"Oh, Teresa, I can't do it. I mean, I think that's not for me."

"Suit yourself," Teresa shrugged. "Why don't you time me? I want to get in another couple of runs."

This time Crystal watched specifically for when Teresa spurred Hawkeye and when she brought down the whip. It was obvious even at a distance that the harder Teresa prodded him the faster he ran. It turned out to be Teresa's best time of the day.

Crystal had a couple more fair runs, but could never force herself to follow the advice Teresa gave her.

"Hey, Lil' Flash, I'm heading in. You want to come on in the house and wait for your dad, or do you want to ride a little more?"

"Uh, I'd kind of like to ride, do you mind?" Crystal responded.

"No sweat, just turn out the lights when you're through. Hey, I'll leave these spurs on the rail, in case you change your mind." Teresa led Hawkeye out of the arena and back into the adjoining barn.

At first, Crystal rode Caleb around the arena at a slow trot. She imagined fans packed into giant stands all around. She even practiced her smile and wave, as if she were rodeo queen. It was awesome to be the only rider.

As she came around the rail by the barn entrance, she spotted the spurs. She decided she should at least try them on. They fit her boots, and as she pranced along the edge of the arena leading Caleb, she enjoyed listening to the jingle.

"If only Patty and Megan could see me now!"

Crystal said of her southern California friends. She glanced down at the old jeans, blue print western shirt, and jeans jacket that she wore. Her brown boots were covered with dirt and dust, and her hat was a little beat up. "They wouldn't even recognize me," she decided to her amusement. "I don't even recognize me!"

Crystal climbed up on Caleb and once again imagined a great crowd all around. She ran through the pole bending routine at a mild trot and took a bow before her make-believe fans.

She trotted Caleb down to the starting line again and then waited for the imaginary announcer. "Ladies and gentlemen, welcome to the Idaho State Finals of High School Rodeo. First, will be Miss Crystal LuAnne Blake of Highland High School. . . ."

Crystal heard the roar go up. She knew what she needed to do. She would spur and whip Caleb on to his fastest time ever, then she would jump off him at the finish line, toss her hat in the air, and wave like a pro.

She walked Caleb around for a moment, approached the starting line, and then kicked him with the spurs. He flew down to the far end of the arena. She paced him back around the poles, each time using the spurs as Teresa had suggested.

It wasn't until she made the turn and started back up the poles that she remembered the quirt. As she pushed Caleb out of the far end of

22

the poles, she spurred him hard and brought the quirt down on the side of his neck. Her hat sailed away as she felt Caleb surge faster than ever before.

Crystal was thinking of how to jump from him after they finished when, suddenly, Caleb stumbled. His right front leg collapsed with a sudden drop and thrust of his right shoulder.

Crystal lost her grip and landed on her face in the dirt. Her first thought was of Caleb, so she shoved her hands in the dirt to lift herself up.

Her left hand collapsed under her, and her face slammed back down into the ground of the empty, indoor arena.

2
THE SECRET ADMIRER

CRYSTAL SCREAMED OUT AT THE SHARP JAB OF pain in her left wrist. She rolled over and sat up by using her right hand for leverage. Caleb was stopped a few feet away. He breathed hard, with foamy saliva dripping from where the bit entered his mouth. Crystal sat in the dust holding her left wrist with her right hand, knowing that tears were running down her dirty cheeks. She searched around the still arena. This was definitely not the way she had envisioned the finale.

She struggled to her feet and limped over to survey Caleb. Holding her injured hand against her body, she took his reins in her right hand and walked slowly towards the barn entrance. Caleb didn't seem to show any signs of injury.

By the time she turned out the lights and led Caleb past the barn area, her now inactive left wrist had settled down to a dull throb. She closed the big arena door and turned to see her dad walking toward her.

He glanced at the dirt, tears, and protected wrist. "I presume you had a little trouble in there," he greeted her.

"I think I was pushing Caleb too fast, or something. Anyway, he stumbled, and I came flying over his head and fell on my wrist. It really hurts. Dad, check out Caleb's right front leg. I hope he didn't get hurt."

Mr. Blake examined Caleb. "He looks better than you. Come on, kiddo, let's get Caleb trailered and see if we can catch the doctor in Craigmont to check out your hand."

It was almost nine that evening before she finished with the doctor, chores, and dinner. Crystal called Shawn from her parents' office phone downstairs.

"Hi, it's me," Crystal reported when she heard Shawn's familiar voice.

"Me who?" he teased.

"Me! You turkey. Remember that foxy chick you can't live without?" she bantered.

"Oh, yeah," he countered, "that cute, little redhead from Kamiah."

"You're dead meat, Shawn Sorensen. Get your will in order, 'cause I won't show any mercy," Crystal retorted.

"I repent, I repent," he pleaded and laughed. "What's up?"

"I took a header with Caleb and sprained my left wrist. Banged it up pretty bad, I guess. The doctor said I'll need to wear a brace for a week or so."

"Does that mean you'll miss the rodeo at Kalispell?" he questioned.

"No way, I'll just have to be careful. I don't

think it will slow down the cutting, but I'm not sure about the barrels and poles."

"Hey, you're tough, you can do it. Besides, we need all the points we can get. There will be five teams up there, and I hear it's been a long time since Highland won."

"You sure sound hyped up—as usual. Listen," Crystal added, "can you go over to the arena tomorrow and watch me and Caleb? I want to make sure he isn't hurt."

"Yeah, sure. The whole team has practice tomorrow. Did you notice any steers around the barn? I need to get in some roping."

"Uh, I really didn't notice. Boy, you should have seen that fall. I've never flown off Caleb like that before."

"Welcome to the real world," Shawn laughed. Then his tone became more serious. "Really, I'm glad you weren't hurt. When something like that happens to me, I figure I can either sit around feeling sorry for myself, or look around and see how God can use it for some benefit—to me or others. You know what I mean?"

"Sure . . . thanks, I needed a better perspective. Sometimes it seems like riding is all that there is in life." Crystal listened to the echo of her own words as she spoke.

"Did Teresa call you tonight?" Shawn asked. "She said she tried and you weren't at home. Anyway, she's decided to have a Christmas vacation party at her house Friday night. She wanted us to come. Can you make it?"

"I'll have to ask, but I think so. I thought you were going down to Riggins?"

"We aren't going until Saturday. . . . Say, do you want to go with us? We'll probably stop by to see Gretchen and Doc," Shawn said.

"Hey, that would be great." Crystal hadn't seen Gretchen more than twice since the wedding. "I'll check it all out with my folks and get back to you tomorrow."

"All right, Hey . . . sweet dreams."

"Bye. Yeah, you, too." Crystal hung up the phone and went back to her room. "What cute, little redhead in Kamiah?" she stewed. "I'll rip her lips out."

Gabrielle met Crystal in the school hallway, first thing the next morning. She bubbled with excitement as she ran toward Crystal.

"Hey, Lil' Flash, wait until you hear about . . . Crystal! What happened to your hand?" Gabrielle's words stumbled over each other as she noticed the brace on Crystal's arm.

"Oh, I took a spill with Caleb at practice yesterday. I mean, I was really whipping it on when he stumbled and I kept going. Anyway, it's just a sprain. But it sure hurt. So what's the news?"

"You won't believe this. . . . It's incredible! I've got a secret admirer," Gabrielle beamed.

"A what?"

"Really, a secret admirer. Yesterday in the

27

mail I got this note. Here, read it." Gabrielle unfolded a well-worn letter that was neatly typed.

" 'You're the greatest.' That's it?" Crystal asked. "Nothing else?"

"Then this morning this was in my locker." Gabrielle reached into her pocket.

"A giant candy kiss?" Crystal giggled.

"And another note. Look, it says, 'Love, your greatest fan.' " Gabrielle pointed to the tiny, typewritten note.

"Wow, do you have any idea who it is?"

"How in the world would I know? I thought maybe you knew of somebody." Gabrielle shoved the notes back into her pocket.

"I can't even guess, but you can eliminate one guy. Shawn. He's mine. So that only leaves fifty-one other boys."

"Half of which are jerks," Gabrielle sighed.

"Hey, a fan is a fan. Don't be picky, at least until he identifies himself," Crystal urged. "You going to practice riding this afternoon?"

"Yeah . . . I really need to." Gabrielle turned toward their classroom. "You want me to drive?"

"Only until a week from Saturday. Then I get my license, and look out, world!"

"Boy, you can say that again; I've seen you drive," Gabrielle laughed.

"All right, that's it. Where's General Miles when you need him?" Crystal elbowed Gabrielle as they headed down the hallway. "Are you going to Teresa's party?"

"Oh, yeah, it sounds great." Gabrielle stopped and looked at Crystal. "Are you going with Shawn?"

"Well, you know . . . my folks won't let me officially date until I'm sixteen. But you could say that Shawn and I are both going to the party," Crystal explained.

"I don't get the sixteen stuff," Gabrielle said.

"I don't mind, really. They just think I shouldn't be burdened with a more serious relationship at age fourteen."

"Fourteen and a half," Gabrielle corrected.

"Yeah, fourteen and a half."

"Well, I can tell you one girl who wouldn't mind being burdened down a little bit," Gabrielle countered. She held out the candy kiss. "Now, I wonder just who this heartsick fool really is?"

"Some seventh grader, no doubt," Crystal kidded.

"You don't really think so . . . do you?"

"Come on, let's get this day over with." Crystal slipped into the classroom and found her chair.

"Look!" Gabrielle pointed to a heart-shaped, red note on her desk. "He struck again! It says, 'I'll see you at the party.' Wow, this is getting serious."

Although Gabrielle floated through the day,

Crystal felt the drudgery of last-minute home-work and exams. She enjoyed relaxing in the truck, gazing out at a frigid, colorless landscape, as they drove out to the arena for rodeo practice after school.

"So different than summer," she yawned. The rolling hills of the 4,000-foot-high Camas Prairie capped miles of frosted grayness. The charcoal-colored clouds blended with shadowed mountains, making it difficult to discern where land and sky separated. Yet there was a cleanness, a stillness, a freshness to winter that she had never experienced before. Crystal thought of it as God's reminder of the different moods and emotions in her own life as well. Each season with its own feel, its own beauty, its own challenge.

"Gabrielle, do you like winter?" Crystal ventured to ask.

"Oh, everyone complains about the cold and the snow. But it's mainly just talk. Anytime we have a brown Christmas, you know, with no snow, those same folks cry for weeks. Really, I don't mind a little wearing-heavy-coats-and-gloves weather as long as there is a warm room to go home to. One winter we lived out near the community of Forest, and we ran out of fire-wood. I thought I'd die of the cold. I used to think up reasons for staying after school."

Crystal changed the subject. "Gabrielle, do you have a lot of riding trophies?"

"Oh, sure, I guess so. Although I've probably

got more ribbons than trophies. Some of the rodeos I compete in can't afford lots of trophies. Why do you ask?"

"Well, it's just Shawn, Teresa . . . you. You've all been around competition so much that I'd think another victory wouldn't seem all that important. Yet, whenever I get around Teresa I get the feeling that she'd do anything to win. I mean, there's more to life than just winning." Crystal pulled her hat down over her eyes and scrunched down in the pickup as they pulled into the Patterson ranch driveway.

"Yeah, like what?" Gabrielle tossed back.

"Well, like being happy and enjoying your family and knowing the Lord and . . ."

"And getting notes from a secret admirer!" Gabrielle whooped. "Listen, Lil' Flash, I figure you're both right and wrong. I mean, all those things are important. But for some people, the arena's about the only place in life where they get a chance to be someone. And if you're second rate there, well, it can be depressing. Listen, whenever you stop trying to be first, you might as well hang it up, you've lost the competitive edge."

"I suppose . . ." Crystal climbed out of the warm truck into the brisk, mountain air.

"Look at you," Gabrielle continued talking as the girls led their horses into the arena. "Do you ever expect to take first place in barrel racing?"

"Yeah, sure . . . I mean someday, someplace

you and Teresa will have a bad day, and I'm going to be right there," Crystal answered.

"Exactly! Now how have your times been coming in the barrels?"

"Oh, I lop off a few tenths every week, I guess," Crystal shurugged.

"Now, do you expect to win first in the pole bending?"

Crystal wasn't sure where Gabrielle was leading. "Oh, not in poles. I'm just not that good. That's how I hurt my arm, you know."

"Have your times been improving in the poles?" Gabrielle prodded.

"Not like the barrels. . . . Like I said . . ."

"That's the point. If you aren't aiming to be the very best, if you don't try your hardest to win every time, you don't improve much. That's my point. If you are going to compete, compete to win."

"All right, cowgirl, you convinced me. Move aside for the next state rodeo champion," Crystal crowed.

"Hah!" Gabrielle kidded, "you'll have to whip me first, yellow hair."

Crystal was careful running Caleb through some warm-ups. She still worried about his stumbling the day before and kept looking for signs of trouble. He seemed to be strong. In fact, Crystal thought he felt really anxious to run.

Still fired up from Gabrielle's lecture, Crystal determined to make this a productive practice.

She pushed Caleb through the cloverleaf barrel course at maximum speed, hat and dust flying. While she waited with the others for another turn, she surveyed Gabrielle's and Teresa's rides, hoping to spot their secrets for making such good times.

"For one thing," Crystal considered, "they approach the barrels much faster. I start slowing down too soon." On the next practice run she resisted slowing Caleb down until the last possible moment. She almost flew off him as he made the cut, but grabbed the horn with both hands and stayed firm in the saddle to the run's finish. It was her best time of the day.

Teresa rode over to Crystal who was walking Caleb back across the arena to retrieve her hat.

"Hey, Crys . . . that was a good ride. What got into you?"

"An Indian pep talk," Crystal bantered. "That, and the fact that I keep finishing so far behind you two. I was afraid that this brace would slow me down. But I guess as long as I don't fall off again, I'll be all right. So, did you hear about Gabrielle's secret admirer?"

"Oh, yeah. Everyone's heard. Don't you think she's going a little overboard with all that? I mean, it's not that big a deal to get a note from some guy."

"Uh, well, I think it is for Gabrielle. I mean, it would be for me, too. I don't get too many anonymous notes, do you?"

Teresa pushed her hat back, "Oh, not many from guys. Sometimes I get threatening notes from jealous girls. It's no big. If all this were a sort of joke . . . well, Gabrielle is setting herself up for a big letdown. You know what I mean?"

"Do you know who's doing this?" Crystal re-mounted Caleb.

"I didn't say that, but I hope she doesn't let this affect her riding. We're going to need every point we can hold onto at Kalispell." Teresa trotted off to the barn area.

Crystal kept thinking about Teresa's words as they finished practice. *If this is some practical joke on Gabrielle, it's sure a cruel one.*

When she and Gabrielle led the horses out to return home it was after dark and cold enough to snow again. They hopped into the truck, started the motor, and flipped on the lights. Gabrielle hollered to Crystal. "Hey, look. He's at it again. Someone scraped the ice off the window in the shape of a heart."

"Yeah, neat. But, if this guy's so serious, why doesn't he let you know who he is? I mean, it's not like you're strangers. You grew up with everyone in the class, right?"

"Sure . . . oh, who knows. He must be someone on the rodeo team. Who else knew my pickup was out here at Pattersons'?"

"Everyone in school knows we come out here. He could have driven up and done it, then driven away," Crystal reported.

34

"Oh, I suppose. Anyway, I'll find out tomorrow night," Gabrielle reminded her.

Crystal was silent for most of the trip back home. She kept getting more and more worried that Gabrielle was in for a big disappointment.

Friday was zilch day at school. That's what Crystal called a day where little was expected, and little was done. It was the day before Christmas vacation started, and all anyone wanted to talk about was Teresa's party. Parties at the Patterson house were known to be first class. The two biggest difficulties Crystal had were trying to keep Gabrielle sane and rational after she discovered another present in her locker and trying to figure out what to wear to the party.

It wasn't until twenty minutes before the party when she decided what to wear.

"I want to wear a dress, but all my dresses are California dresses," she whined at her mother as they stood peering into the closet. "Gosh, I sound just like Karla, don't I?"

"It's a feminine characteristic," her mother laughed and dug through some more of Crystal's clothes. "I think you'd better stick to a skirt and sweater. How about the long skirt so you can wear those new dressy boots that Grandma sent?"

"No way . . . that's too . . . you know, old-fashioned looking. I wouldn't be caught dead in that skirt."

"It makes you look long legged," her mother said matter-of-factly.

"Really?"

Fifteen minutes later Crystal arrived at the Pattersons' dressed in the long skirt, lacy white blouse, and boots. Teresa greeted her at the door wearing a long-sleeved, tight-fitting, turquoise blouse covered with shimmering, little mirrored discs that twinkled as she walked across the room. A deep scoop neck and a catlike smile completed the picture.

The room was starting to fill up. Crystal and Gabrielle strolled over to the punch bowl that was near an elegantly decorated Christmas tree.

"Her blouse is too low," Crystal whispered.

"On Teresa, it doesn't make any difference," Gabrielle countered. "Hey, I wish my admirer would hurry up and make a move."

"Maybe you're just as well off not knowing," Crystal suggested as she picked up something that looked like a miniature pecan pie and popped it into her mouth.

Gabrielle motioned, "Let's sit over here by the fireplace and give the guy a chance to spot me."

Crystal and Gabrielle proceeded to rate all the contenders in the room as they whispered and munched cookies. "Not Leon," Gabrielle reported, "I don't think he can even write."

"How about Eddie Valentine?" Crystal asked.

"No way, his dad's always putting down Indians."

"There's J.T. He's a good roper," Crystal suggested.

"Oh, no, not J.T. He was my boyfriend when I was in the sixth grade, but he dumped me."

"How come?"

"Because I didn't like to chew tobacco."

Crystal went down the line of guests. "And it can't be Richard, because he's been chasing Mindy, and Paul is going with Becky, and Chad likes Barbara."

"And Jud is going with his computer," Gabrielle laughed.

"Hey, maybe it is Jud. Just because he studies a lot . . ."

"Jud! Oh, no! Dork City! Tell me it isn't Jud." Gabrielle faked despair.

"Well, I don't know . . . maybe the dude's not here tonight. There come Shawn and Travis. You know it's not them. Carolyn, over at Nezperce, is latched onto Travis."

"That leaves Shawn," Gabrielle kidded.

"Shawn? Shawn who?" Crystal pretended innocence.

It was a great party. Crystal spent most of the night laughing. They played a long game of charades, and Teresa proved to be the biggest ham in the group. When the game finished, most headed for the punch bowl, while Crystal looked for Shawn. He was nowhere in sight. She tiptoed toward the Patterson den, where most of the guys ended up, and noticed someone out in the entryway sorting through the coats that were piled on a love-seat.

She recognized Shawn's profile and started to call to him. But she shut her mouth when she saw him stuff something in a coat pocket, then stalk off to the den. She hurried over to the coats and picked up hers. Though she searched both pockets, she found nothing. She laid it back down, and as she did, brushed against Gabrielle's coat, feeling something in her pocket. She looked up to see if anyone was watching, then pulled a little square box out of Gabrielle's coat.

"A present? A present from Shawn to Gabrielle? Is he . . . ?" Suddenly Crystal felt very, very sick.

3
A SUDDEN CHINOOK

CRYSTAL DECIDED AGAINST GOING INTO THE DEN. She returned to the Patterson living room on legs that felt like wood. She collapsed into a big, leather chair with a groan. Suddenly it all made sense, Crystal thought. "Shawn really likes Gabrielle. She is a lot better at riding, and she can rope. Besides that, she's really cute and independent and . . . and that's why all the secrecy! He couldn't reveal himself to Gabrielle until he broke up with me," she stewed.

"Well, if that's the way he is, maybe it's about time I found out. I'm not going to have everyone laughing at me. . . ." Crystal felt her face muscles tighten. "What am I saying? This doesn't have to be the end. I'll give her a fight. No one's going to horn in on my . . . why, I ought to . . ." Crystal searched for appropriate retaliation. She thought for a minute, then didn't know whether to laugh, cry, or pray. Her indecision was interrupted.

"Hey, Lil' Flash!" It was Gabrielle. "Have you seen Shawn? I'm looking for him."

"What for?" Crystal snapped.

"Huh? Is something bothering you? You go find him then, but Mr. Patterson wants him."

Gabrielle scooted back across the room. Crystal felt trapped in a daze. It was strange how lonely the last five minutes had made her feel. She realized that most of her contentment in moving to Idaho and entering a new school was tied up with her two friends, Gabrielle and Shawn. If she didn't have them, she really was all alone.

She was still staring at Gabrielle, but her mind continued to fly. It had always been all right if the three of them did things together. She and Shawn, and Gabrielle tagging along. Crystal liked it that way. But she couldn't bear thinking about Gabrielle and Shawn, and her the one who was tagging along. Suddenly she began to sense what Gabrielle must have been feeling all along. Then she did start to cry.

Crystal got up and walked over to the beautiful Christmas tree. It was a blue spruce decorated with nothing but silver ornaments hanging from navy blue, velvet ribbons. As Crystal stared at the tree she prayed, "Lord, I really need to have Shawn and Gabrielle for friends. . . . Help me not to lose them."

Then she remembered to go find Shawn. She dried her eyes and headed for the den. Several of the boys, including Shawn, were pouring over a scrapbook of rodeo memoirs.

"Hey, look at this one. Look, there's Mr. Patterson riding Little Midnight."

"He rode Little Midnight?"

"Took the silver at Calgary, 1962."

"Shawn," Crystal called.

"Hey, come look at this . . . look at this trophy he won at Houston. Really, All Around Cowboy, 1960!"

"Shawn!"

"Oh . . . Crys . . . look at this. Wow, Mr. Patterson knew them all, I mean, knows them all."

"Well, Mr. Patterson is looking for you, but I really don't know where he is. Anyway, I was just bringing the message," Crystal stammered.

"He must be out in the barn still. . . . You ought to see the tack he's got out .there. It's incredible! I'll grab Gabrielle. . . . Say, do you want to come out, too? It's kind of cold." Shawn headed back toward the living room.

"Would you rather I didn't go?" Crystal asked with a sinking feeling.

"Oh, you can go; it's just that it's freezing, and all that's out there is a bunch of rodeo gear. I didn't think you were interested. That's why Gabrielle and I were out there."

"You were?"

"Yeah, and it was really neat."

"It was?"

"Listen, Mr. Patterson dug out this pair of silver spurs that he won at a rodeo down in Tucson. I mean, it's a gorgeous, engraved pair, and he gave those suckers to me. Would you believe it? Come on, let me show them to you."

Shawn headed for the entryway. "I went out there without my coat last time, and just about died. I stuck those spurs in my coat pocket; there is no way I wanted to lose them."

"In your coat pocket?" Crystal echoed. "Is your coat piled there on the love seat?"

"Sure, just like all the rest. Here it is, next to yours. Look at these babies. Aren't they something?" Shawn pulled out the gleaming spurs and let Crystal hold them.

"You mean you were putting spurs in your pocket, not a present in Gabrielle's?" Crystal stopped, hesitant to reveal her fears.

"Gabrielle's? Present? Why would I . . . I mean, you didn't think that I . . . me? You think I am Gabrielle's secret . . ."

"No, no, but really, I . . . there is a present in Gabrielle's pocket, and when I saw you over here, I assumed . . . I'm a jerk, aren't I?" Crystal finished softly with head down.

"A little insecure, maybe, but not a jerk," Shawn laughed. "You want to bundle up and go out to the tack room?"

"Actually, I'd rather stay by the fire."

"Good, how about getting me a hot cup of cider? I'll be right back."

Crystal prepared two cups of cider and stuck a stick of cinnamon in hers. Then, she sat down next to Mrs. Patterson.

"You sure have a beautiful Christmas tree," Crystal began.

42

"Thanks, Crystal. Trish found that little spruce down toward the river. Of course, the ornaments come from the silver mine. Back in the thirties, silver prices were next to nothing, and we had this Austrian silversmith stop by our house looking for work. Well, my dad gave him room and board if he would make us some decorations for the tree. Aren't they something? It's kind of one of those fluke deals that come along."

"They must be worth a lot."

"Well, we always kid that we could sell the ornaments and send the girls to college. How's this cold weather treating you California natives?" Mrs. Patterson smiled.

"We really like it. I mean, our whole family gets out in the snow and sleds and stuff. We all enjoy . . ."

"Look, here comes the cold couple." Mrs. Patterson glanced at Shawn and Gabrielle who were knocking a little snow off their coats and shoes as they reentered the house.

Shawn headed toward Crystal, but Gabrielle lagged back in the entryway.

"Crys, look at this! Oh, hi, Mrs. Patterson. Look what Mr. Patterson had. An extra pair of woolly chaps. Great, huh?"

Crystal peered at the slightly worn, dirty, white wool chaps that smelled like a wet goat. "Uh, yeah, that's great."

"Boy, I appreciate the things he's given me,

43

Mrs. Patterson. You folks sure are generous."

"Well, Shawn, Stan never left the rodeo tour at heart. He still thinks that he's traveling on down the road. And when he comes across a young guy like you, with all your potential, I kind of think he wishes he had a son or two. So you wear those chaps some cold day and win some silver. That'll hype Stan up for a month."

"Crystal! Crys . . . come here a minute." Gabrielle was calling to her from the entryway.

Crystal carried her now lukewarm cider over to Gabrielle. "What's up? Did you get some woolly chaps, too?"

"Oh, no. I mean, I did get a nice pair of spurs that Mrs. Patterson wore in the Cow Palace one time. But look! I found it in my pocket when I went out to the barn, but I didn't open it till just now. It's a silver locket. Inside it says, 'You're the one.' "

"But why still the secrecy? I thought he would, you know, reveal himself tonight?" Crystal questioned.

"Yeah, that's what I thought. Anyway, I hope he does something soon; it's about time to go home. This is really fun, but it's starting to get on my nerves." Gabrielle gave the whole room another once-over.

By the time Crystal's dad arrived to give the girls a ride back to Winchester, Gabrielle still had not discovered the identity of her secret admirer. So the two rode back in silence.

44

When they reached the outskirts of town Gabrielle turned to Crystal and spoke softly. "You know, Crys, a year ago I never would have gone to that party. I mean, I was just too self-conscious about being the only Indian kid in school. But now, with a good friend like you, I'm starting to feel like I really belong. You know what I mean? Oh, anyway, it probably sounds crazy. . . . You always fit in everywhere. It's the curse of cute blondes, I guess."

Crystal didn't look Gabrielle in the eye as she got out of the truck and started for the front door. Crystal didn't want her friend to see the tears.

Mr. Blake drove on up the snow-crusted, gravel road and parked in front of the Blake house. The outdoor lights illuminated the raised wooden sidewalk that zigzagged up the incline to the front door. The air was freezing, yet Crystal felt invigorated and renewed as she walked up the steps with her dad.

"You know what, Dad? I'm learning that having good friends might just be the neatest thing in the whole world," she said as she grabbed his arm.

He gave her a hug as they scooted through the front door.

Crystal had just finished breakfast on Saturday morning when Shawn and his folks pulled into the driveway. She was looking forward to going down to Riggins with them. It would be her first time to visit some of Shawn's old friends, and she hoped they could call on Gretchen and Doc, too.

She still wore a brace on her arm from the spill a few days before, and she had bundled up in jeans, heavy parka, and moon boots. As they started across the prairie and began the descent to the Salmon River Canyon, the wind began to howl.

"Looks like a Chinook," Mr. Sorensen commented.

"A what?" Crystal said, puzzled.

"Every so often we get a hot wind that blows down right in the middle of winter. The temperature rises about sixty to eighty degrees, the snows melt, the rivers run high, and you'd think it was springtime. Then, in just a matter of minutes, it can drop right back down even colder than before. By the time we get to Riggins you two will wish you were in shorts."

The idea of an eighty-degree jump in temperature in just minutes sounded unbelievable to Crystal, but she did notice that by the time they reached Riggins she had discarded coat, gloves, and boots. It was plain hot.

"Dad, you can let Crystal and me out at the store. We'll grab a drink, and then I want her to meet some friends. Could you just stop back at Gretchen's later this afternoon?" Shawn requested.

"OK, we'll be down at your Aunt Melissa's. You two stay out of trouble, you hear?" he responded with a friendly grin.

Crystal had passed through the town of Riggins often, but never stopped. She couldn't tell if she liked the place or not. It seemed to cling to the canyon walls where the Little Salmon and the central fork of the Salmon merged. The two channels turned northward for the final journey before they plunged into the Snake River. Riggins was the jumping off place for fishermen and white-water rafting enthusiasts. Other than that, she could see little reason for its existence.

As she and Shawn entered the store, Crystal encountered one of the most attractive girls she had ever seen working at the checkout stand. She had a good figure, flashy eyes, and gorgeous, long, blonde, curly hair. She wore old blue jeans and a flannel shirt tied at her waist, but she definitely looked uptown.

"Shawn!" the girl called when she saw them enter.

Crystal was afraid she had met this girl before . . . somewhere in a bad dream.

Shawn walked up to the girl. "Crys, this is Terri Biggers. I think I mentioned her to you before."

Terri looked Crystal up and down. "This must be your little Crystal. Brad's told me all about you." Then she dismissed Crystal with a quick toss of her head and turned to Shawn, "You going to be in town long?"

"No," Crystal broke in and grabbed Shawn by the arm, dragging him toward the door. "We're only here for a few hours. Nice meeting you though." She gave a determined effort at a parting smile.

"Your 'little Crystal'!" she fumed. "Did you hear that . . . that. . . . She makes Teresa seem like a saint."

"Well, she does look a little different," Shawn stammered. "It's funny how quickly girls start to . . . you know, grow up."

"Yeah, I don't think I want a drink. Let's go."

They started down the sidewalk when they heard a familiar voice holler, "Shawn! Crystal! Hey, wait up!"

It was Brad Paller. "Hey, what's happenin'? You two lost?"

Shawn slapped Brad on the back. "You won any silver lately?"

"A little, and you?" Brad questioned.

"At Pendleton High School, about a month or so ago, did I tell you about that?" Shawn leaned against a black pickup parked at the curb.

"Oh, yeah. Hey, do you two want to go up the river? I've got the boat out, what with this blast of hot air I was thinking about a spin."

"Crys, have you ever been on a jet boat?"

"No, but that sounds great. Is it safe?" she added.

48

"You bet," Brad assured. "Listen, I was just headed in to see if Terri could go. We can make it a foursome."

"Uh oh, sorry, Brad. I forgot to mention we've got to get down to Gretchen's. We just won't be able to go," Crystal said rapidly.

"Crystal's met Terri, I take it," Brad laughed. "Terri has, er . . . matured a little since last summer, wouldn't you say, Shawn?" Brad winked.

"I guess it happens to all of us," Shawn ventured. "You sure you don't want to go?"

"Really, I do want to see Gretchen," Crystal repeated.

Shawn and Crystal strolled across the street to Delia's Dairy Delight, bought a cold drink, and sat down at one of the outside tables. Crystal tried to feel Shawn out. "Did you see those atrocious fingernails? They didn't even match her outfit."

"Are you talking about Terri? She had fingernails?" Shawn teased.

They finished their drinks and the tour of beautiful, downtown Riggins about the same time, then hiked south along the state highway next to the Little Salmon.

"There used to be a lumber mill across the road there." Shawn pointed.

"Yeah, and I'll bet it burned down under very mysterious circumstances, right?" Crystal snickered.

"Well, not exactly. Last June it was hit by lightning and burned right to the ground. I guess they'll wait for better lumber prices before they build it back up. There's no mystery about lightning, except why it hits one building and not another. My dad says only the Lord understands weather . . . and women," Shawn laughed.

"Hah! How about men? They can sure drive you crazy sometimes . . . especially the cowboy variety."

"My, are you talking about anyone I know?" Shawn reached out and grabbed Crystal's hand as they turned into the driveway of a small but immaculate, white, clapboard house. "Let's see if Gretchen and Doc are home."

Gretchen met them at the door with a big holler and a hug. "Crystal! Shawn! I'm glad you stopped by. Another day and you would have missed us."

"You going on vacation?" Crystal inquired as she sat down on a chair that looked like an antique.

"Doc's gone down to Boise to make some arrangements. We're flying to his place in Florida on Monday. Thought we'd spend a few weeks down there. It's mean, dirty, rotten work, but someone has to enjoy all that Florida sun," she chuckled.

"Hey, it's hot here in Riggins," Crystal noted.

"Sure, as long as the Chinook blows. But it

won't be long before we're stoking up the wood stove again. Can I get you two a sandwich? I was about to fix a little lunch and then go take care of the horses."

"Only if you let us work for our lunch," Shawn volunteered. "We'll help you with the stock."

In a matter of minutes the three sat around a highly varnished redwood table that served as Gretchen's kitchen table. She had homemade bread, sliced meat and cheese, home-canned pickles, and a bowl of potato chips waiting for them.

"How's married life, Gretchen? Is it really like you thought it would be?" Crystal asked.

"Nope," she scowled.

"It's not?" Crystal sputtered.

"It's even better," Gretchen affirmed with a jovial wave of the hand. "You two know how long I was single. Well, I want to tell you I've tried both, and for me being married is about 1000 times better. 'Course I could be prejudiced. I think I got one of the last truly great men."

"I hope there's one or two left," Crystal interjected.

"Not my age, honey." Gretchen paused to lead them in a blessing before they tore into lunch.

Crystal glanced at Gretchen as she ate. She was, on the surface, middle aged, stocky, and tough skinned from years of range work. But her eyes reflected a heart that was young, sensitive, and full of adventure.

"How's that horse of yours treating you?" Gretchen broke into the silence.

"Caleb? Oh, he's great. Independent, ornery, and stubborn as always, but he's great. Did you know I've been using him in the cutting event? He's won every time."

"That doesn't surprise me one bit. He's a cow pony if I ever saw one. How about the barrels?"

"Well, I'm really improving, but I need to find a way to pick up my time a little to ever have a chance of winning. That's how I hurt this arm. I tried to spur Caleb a little, and I guess I didn't know what I was doing. I sailed right off him."

"Have you got a pair of spurs?"

"Not really, I was just borrowing Teresa's," Crystal replied.

"In that case, I've got a pair you can use. They can be a real help sometimes. It all depends on the type of spur, and on the horse. Some horses just don't like the feel of them. After lunch let's go out back to the corral, and I'll show you how to use them."

Shawn tended some of the livestock while Gretchen and Crystal saddled up a white-quarter horse mare.

"She'll do a good job on the cloverleaf pattern," Gretchen announced, "and she won't complain about a spur or two. Warm her up a little and then give me your best ride without the spurs. Don't worry if it's not as fast as Caleb.

Old Honeypot there is about ten years older than you are, and her legs aren't what they used to be. But she did run in Cheyenne once."

Crystal liked the feel of the big, white horse. She was quick, and yet, gentle, too. Crystal ran a couple of rounds with Gretchen timing her.

"That last one went pretty good," Crystal called out. "She's a neat old horse."

"Honey, I didn't say she was old. She's just . . . mature," Gretchen corrected. "Now, try on these spurs."

"Oh, those are different than Teresa's. Hers had longer little wheels."

"Rowels. She uses long rowels? No wonder Caleb complained. Anyway, just one sharp jab as you start each straightaway, and a couple down the finish, you'd be surprised how much better your times will be."

Crystal ran six rounds with the big, white horse and every time they were two to four seconds quicker than without the spurs. She was happy to be carrying the spurs home with her.

The Sorensens pulled into Gretchen's driveway about three. Shawn and Crystal said their good-byes and loaded up.

It was a quiet ride up the canyon to the top of the mountains and the 4,000-foot Camas Prairie. Near the city of White Bird the dark clouds started to roll across the sky, stacking up on the mountains to the east.

"Say good-bye to your brief touch of warm

weather," Mrs. Sorensen nodded. "Looks like the Chinook has passed."

A few minutes later, Shawn began quietly to chuckle.

"What's that all about?" Crystal whispered.

"Now you've met Terri Biggers," he grinned.

"Yeah. I guess I wasn't all that nice."

"Well, I've been thinking a lot about both of you this afternoon." He averted his eyes out the window.

"You have?"

"Sure. And I figured out why I like you so much better."

"You do?"

"Yeah."

"Why?"

" 'Cause of all the dumb things you say and do." He turned to look straight at her. "See, most girls I know are always trying to be something different. Always covering up what they really feel. I get exhausted just trying to figure out what they are really after. But not you. You are so transparent. It doesn't matter whether you're sad, happy, jealous, depressed, or excited. It all comes right out. I know how to react to that. Don't ever change, OK?"

She nodded and looked out at the oncoming storm. She had never noticed before how great a person could feel, even on a very gloomy day.

4
AN UNSUITABLE DISCOVERY

CRYSTAL LAY IN HER BED AND STARED AT THE ceiling. She thought about her pet theory about time. There was slow time, and there was fast time. Both had sixty minutes in an hour, but some hours had fast minutes and some slow minutes. Now if you had a run of fast minutes, your life whizzed by. But there didn't seem to be any way to predict when those fast minutes would strike. They just sort of blew down out of nowhere like that strange Chinook wind.

If that's true, Crystal thought, *then I've just been hit with a three-day siege of fast minutes.* It was Wednesday morning—still five days until Christmas. Since she'd gone down to Riggins, three quick days had flashed by.

On Sunday, she attended church, rode with Gabrielle after lunch, and in the evening sang in the annual church Christmas program. On Monday, Mr. Peters called to say that he was going to be out of town later in the week and wanted to have the last driver's training lesson and test on Tuesday. That meant Crystal might be able to get her driver's license before she went to the rodeo in Montana.

Crystal, Karla, and Mrs. Blake spent all day Monday down in Lewiston Christmas shopping. Crystal was now through, except for gifts for Shawn and Gabrielle.

On Monday night, Crystal studied the vehicle code until almost midnight so she could pass the written test. Tuesday found her and eight other fourteen-year-olds driving across the frozen prairie of northern Idaho, then packed into a stuffy classroom taking a practice driver's test.

She had been so busy she had hardly seen Shawn or Gabrielle for three days. Gabrielle had called Monday night to say she received a beautiful card signed, "See you in Montana."

Now it was Wednesday, and Crystal wondered if it would be fast time or slow time. Her dad had promised to take her to the sheriff's office at the courthouse in Nezperce for her driver's test. Then, she would hurry home to get packed, because at 2:00, the Highland High School rodeo team would aim for Kalispell, Montana.

"I think I'll pull all my hair back and pin it to my head," Crystal mentioned to Karla as the sisters sat at the breakfast table. "Maybe it will seem like I'm something besides a flighty blonde kid."

"You nervous about the driver's test?" Karla asked.

"Yeah. Were you nervous when you got yours?"

"I sure was. Of course, I had to drive on southern California freeways and down the city streets of L.A. It can't be too hard around Nezperce," Karla encouraged.

"I don't know. I mean, I did everything all right for Mr. Peters, but I'm used to him. What if I panic with a stranger?"

"If you don't pass, you can wait a couple of weeks and take it again," Karla reminded her.

"If I flunk, I'll just die! I've been bragging to Megan and Patty that I would have my license by Christmas. Do you think I'll have to parallel park? I don't do too well with parallel parking."

"Oh, yeah, I had to parallel park," Karla said. "But you'll do just fine. Don't mess up your hair. You look great as you are—really."

Thirty minutes later Crystal and her dad headed across the rolling prairie to the Lewis County Courthouse at Nezperce. She hardly said a word. In her lap Crystal held a study copy of the vehicle code. She didn't read it, but stared out at the scattered snowflakes blowing in the breeze.

"A lousy day for taking a driving test," Crystal mumbled.

"You worried about all this, princess?" Mr. Blake spoke up.

"Yeah . . . well, it's one of those things that you just aren't sure you can do when it comes right down to doing it. I'm tempted to have you take me back home. I don't think I'm able to handle failure."

"Hey, remember when you first learned to ride a bike without training wheels? You were excited and scared both at the same time. Well, this is the same. You did all that should have been done, so trust your ability to use the skills needed. Mr. Peters wouldn't have signed the release if he weren't confident you could pass."

"Well, I hope I get someone nice to give me the test."

"Here we are, kiddo, beautiful, downtown Nezperce." Mr. Blake parked the pickup in front of the sheriff's office.

Inside they walked down the hallway to a glass-enclosed room at the end of a short hallway. A lady in a sheriff's department uniform conversed on a two-way radio in front of her. When she finished, she greeted them. "Let me guess," she smiled, "you're from Mr. Peters's driver's training class, and you want to take your test, right?"

"How'd you guess?" Crystal blurted.

"You're the fifth one this morning," she replied. "Usually I don't have that many in a week in a county of only 4,000 people. Do you have your papers from Mr. Peters?"

"Sure, here."

"Fill out this form, and both you and your dad will have to sign."

Crystal printed every entry with care. "I think everything's here," she said sheepishly to the lady, whose name tag read "Beverly."

"OK, young lady, here's your test. You can take all the time you need. Just use that counter over there. Remember, no cheating. I've got to go cook some lunch."

"Lunch?" Mr. Blake responded.

"Oh, I'm the sheriff's dispatcher, the vehicle license clerk, the secretary, and the cook for the county jail. It's a very small county," Beverly shrugged, then sauntered into the adjoining glass-walled kitchen and started rummaging in the cupboards. "Just holler when you're through."

The written test wasn't too bad. Crystal had taken several sample tests that were quite similar. In less than ten minutes she was through.

"Ma'am? I'm all finished." Crystal stood at the doorway watching the woman stir a pot on the stove.

"Listen, you come stir this, and I'll grade your test."

"Why, sure, no problem."

Five minutes later Beverly returned to the kitchen carrying some papers. "Thanks," she said as she took the wooden spoon back. "Now I'll cover this mess and let it simmer. Here, I'll need your signature on this paper."

Crystal signed.

"All right, Crystal LuAnne Blake, if you've got $10, you've got a license."

"Huh?"

"You passed. You didn't miss a one. Now, this

is just your temporary license. Let's step back into my office and get your picture for the permanent one. You'll have to give me a profile since you're under sixteen." She walked back toward the hallway.

"Uh, ma'am," Crystal began, "I didn't take the driving part of the test. Don't you need to go out and watch me drive around?"

"You passed Mr. Peters's class, didn't you?"

"Sure."

"Well, that's good enough for me. Now, step up here and read this eye chart. Top line."

"Er, E. P. R. Z. You mean, I really got my license?" Crystal repeated.

"Fourth line. That's right. Remember, it's daytime driving only, until you're sixteen."

"A. F. L. C. S. Really! I did it?" Crystal almost shouted.

"Now, if you'd stand on that line and look at the door to the right."

"Like this? Daddy, did you hear that I got my license?" Crystal called to her father.

"I heard it. Everyone in the building heard it. Your mother back in Winchester probably heard it," her dad chided.

Crystal signed the final paper and headed back out the front door of the sheriff's office. "May I drive home?"

"I guess you need to start sometime." Mr. Blake handed her the keys.

Crystal eased to a stop sign on the outskirts of

Nezperce that read "Rolling right turn, OK."
She slowed, kept going, and turned right. Suddenly, a red light flashed behind her.

"Daddy, there's a policeman. What should I do?"

"Just pull over and see what he wants. Show him your temporary driver's license."

"Me? I don't have it. Don't you have it?" she cried.

"Crystal, it's *your* license. You mean you didn't pick it up off the counter?" By then the officer had walked up to the window on Crystal's side of the car.

"Driving without a license, I see." It was Sergeant Kingman.

Crystal relaxed at the familiar face. "Oh, Sergeant Kingman, boy, am I glad it's you. See, I just got my license, and I forgot to pick up the papers in the sheriff's office. And I . . ."

Sergeant Kingman held out some papers. "You mean these? That's why I pulled you over. Beverly said you rushed off without them. I thought you might want to at least hold onto them until you got home."

Crystal thanked him, then started up the pickup.

"Well, kiddo, you made it three blocks before you were pulled over," Mr. Blake kidded. "That's got to be a record."

It was a hectic two hours of packing all of her clothes and all of Caleb's gear, but by 1:55 Crystal and her dad were at the Pattersons' barn where the rodeo team was to meet.

In less than half an hour, the entire team drove down the road. The caravan included several huge horse trailers, a couple smaller ones, two travel homes, and a half-dozen cars. Crystal, Shawn, Gabrielle, Dusty, and Travis rode with Teresa and her mother in the Pattersons' travel home.

This was the first rodeo that Crystal had gone to where her dad hadn't been along. It felt funny to say good-bye and ride off. Crystal felt her stomach churn.

"Hey, have any of you guys been to this winter rodeo before? I mean, what's it like?" she blurted out.

"I was there last year," Travis spoke up. "They have about five teams there and . . ."

"Where are they from?" Crystal interrupted. "I hope they aren't all as good as Pendleton was. I suppose coming from Montana, they're all pros."

"If it's the same as last year, they'll be from Kalispell, Eureka, Libby, probably an Indian team from Browning."

"Hey, Gabrielle, did you hear that?"

"Forget it, Lil' Flash. Those are Blackfeet. Know what I mean?"

"Uh, well, anyway. What else happens?" Crystal turned back to Travis who was resting on a narrow, little bench, with his black hat pulled way down over his eyes.

"Let's see, we will probably stay out at Glacier Village Motel. It's up toward Glacier National Park. You ever been up there? It's a great place in the summertime. Too cold now. Anyway, the arena is east of town. It's about twice the size of the Pattersons'. It's not the Cow Palace, mind you, but it's not bad."

"Forget about the arena, how's the motel? Do they have a movie channel, or an indoor, heated pool?" Dusty asked.

"Oh, yeah. Both. Listen, that pool is something." Travis looked around at the others. "Did you guys remember your suits?"

"Swimsuits? In Montana? In December? You've got to be kidding. You guys are kidding me, right?" Crystal squealed.

"Don't worry, Lil' Flash," Teresa broke in, "I brought a couple. You can borrow one of mine."

"Then tomorrow and Friday, we rodeo all day. And I do mean *all day*. We're out at the arena from about 7:00 a.m. until 9:00 at night. On Friday are the finals and the closing barbecue. It's really a big deal. Then Saturday we're home. Providing the Lolo Pass doesn't blow closed."

"What happens if it does?" Crystal asked.

"No big deal, we just eat the horses and camp out in the snow on the Locsha," he smiled.

Dusty threw a pillow at Travis, knocking his hat off.

The trip up the Clearwater River, then the

Locsha River, took longer than Crystal had imagined. She and Gabrielle commandeered the backseat in the travel home and watched the caravan out the back window.

"Did I tell you about the note on my door this morning?" Gabrielle asked.

"No. Was it from him?"

"Yeah. Look. 'Win it all at Kalispell.' Signed, 'your A. A. C.' "

"A. A. C., Gabrielle, what's that?"

"All Around Cowboy. You know, like Shawn did at Pendleton."

"Well, it's not Shawn," Crystal reported. "I asked him."

"You did?"

"Yeah, er . . . I . . . well, you know, I just wanted to find out who this was. So who do you think this All Around Cowboy could be?" Crystal whispered so the others couldn't hear. "Hey, everybody, I've got an announcement, listen!"

"Crystal, shhhh, don't . . ." Gabrielle protested.

"Listen, I got busy and forgot to tell you. I passed my driver's test today. I, Crystal LuAnne Blake, am a duly licensed driver."

"Look out, pedestrians," Gabrielle laughed.

Just as suddenly, Crystal put her head close to Gabrielle's again and resumed her hushed conversation. "So who's the All Around Cowboy?"

"The only one I know of, besides Shawn, is Leon."

64

"Leon? He's a senior!" Crystal hissed.

"Yeah, and he chews tobacco and can't spell his name."

"Then it's not Leon. All of these notes have had good spelling."

"Right. Well, if I don't find out by the end of this rodeo, I'm going to stir up the whole team. I don't intend to go through the whole vacation wondering. It's getting weird. Really." Gabrielle closed her eyes and sighed. "Maybe we can sleep off a few miles."

They crossed the state line into Montana; it didn't look any different than Idaho to Crystal. The same threatening clouds. The same mixture of woods and prairie. They grabbed hamburgers in Missoula, then wound their way around Flathead Lake toward Kalispell. At 8:30 they finally rolled into the motel parking lot. The men took the horses out to arena areas, while the women attempted to settle the team into their rooms and ordered pizza in for dinner.

Crystal, Gabrielle, Dusty, and Teresa were to share room 234. Teresa unloaded her suitcase and then disappeared down the hallway.

"Where's Teresa going?" Crystal asked Dusty.

"She's headed out to the arena for some practice," Dusty informed her.

"Tonight? It's late," Crystal replied.

"Sure, but you know Teresa. She's really been working for this rodeo. Do you know she's been in the arena about ten hours a day for the last

65

week?" Dusty sat on the edge of the queen-sized bed next to the television. "Can we have this bed?"

"Sure, me and Lil' Flash will take the one next to the heater," Gabrielle added.

"What does Teresa hope to gain at this rodeo?" Crystal inquired.

"Gabrielle sort of shut her down at Pendleton. Teresa expects to win the All Around award at every rodeo. Anything less than that is failure to her. You know what I mean?"

"Sort of. Why does she push herself like that?"

"I think she keeps trying to please her dad. When you've got a famous rodeo dad who had no sons, well, you sorta get to driving yourself."

"Teresa's really good. But Gabrielle can rope, too. It might be hard to beat her," Crystal added.

"Let alone five other teams," Gabrielle commented.

"Well, she thinks Gabrielle is the one to beat. You'd better watch out she doesn't spike your toothpaste," Dusty commented. "I mean, don't tell her I said this. We've been friends for a long time, but when she gets her mind set on winning she doesn't always act too rationally. If there's any way to do it, she'll try to psyche you out."

Gabrielle and Dusty helped carry up the pizza while Crystal sat on the bed thinking over what Dusty just said. If Teresa was determined to beat Gabrielle, she might try any tactic to keep her from doing her best. "Even," Crystal speculated to herself, "even fake some notes to keep Gabrielle's mind off the rodeo!"

After they gulped down their pizza, most of the team headed for the indoor, heated pool.

"You going swimming, Lil' Flash?" Gabrielle called as she danced out of the bathroom dressed in a deep purple bathing suit and a white, terry-cloth top.

"Yeah, I guess I'll look for a suit in Teresa's things. She said I could borrow one."

Dusty held up some samples. "Here they are, Crystal, take your pick."

Crystal retreated to the bathroom to try them on. One was a light blue string bikini. "Definitely not my color," Crystal grimaced as she held it up to her body in the mirror. She called out to the others, "Does Teresa really wear this blue one?"

"Oh, yeah," Dusty hollered back.

"In public?"

"Only when there are boys around," Dusty called.

"Wow, look at this one." Crystal came out wearing a sea green suit. "I mean it comes way up on my, er . . . and this loose-weave top sort of shows . . . I can't wear this."

"Hey," Dusty commented, "so you give the guys a thrill. Big deal."

"Yeah, well. I mean it's OK for Teresa. It's her choice. But I kinda like to save parts of me from speculation. You know what I mean?"

"Sure, no sweat. Come on down to the pool anyway. Everyone will be there." Gabrielle and Dusty raced out of the room and down the hallway.

Crystal put back on her jeans and shirt and returned the swim wear to Teresa's suitcase. As she did, she noticed a red ball-point pen and a couple of new greeting cards. She picked them up and read them.

"Definitely to be given to a girl, and neither has been signed. And Gabrielle's last note was in red ink!" she exclaimed.

—————————— 5 ——————————

WINNERS AND LOSERS

*T*eresa!" Crystal almost shouted into the empty motel room. *If Teresa is really so possessed with winning, like Dusty says. And if she would do anything to psyche out her opponents. And if Gabrielle is the one she fears competing against the most . . . then. . . .* Crystal got furious just thinking about it.

Gabrielle doesn't need a joke like this. "This is a mean, rotten, dirty thing to do. Teresa, you jerk." Crystal scowled into the mirror as she spoke. "You sit out there in your big ranch house, with your own private arena and money running out of your boots. You've got everything in the world, and Gabrielle has nothing but a little, crowded mill house and a sorrow-filled heritage. I ought to . . . I ought to . . ." Crystal searched for some appropriate expression.

She couldn't think of anything. "If I expose the whole thing, then everybody will laugh at Gabrielle for getting so excited about nothing. If I let this go on, Gabrielle will get hurt when Teresa blows the whistle or just drops the whole thing."

She decided not to go down by the pool, but wait in the room for Teresa to return and confront her with the evidence. She sat on the edge of the queen-sized bed and rolled back the dark green, printed bedspread. She propped up some pillows and lay back against them, rehearsing the big scene that was to come.

The more she thought about it, the madder she got. "No wonder we couldn't figure it out. We kept thinking it was a guy. It's not right to play with someone's emotions like that!"

Crystal leaned over to the nightstand and groped for a switch. She twisted the light on and picked up a Gideon Bible that was lying next to the light. She flipped through the pages looking for a passage to catch her eye. On the back side of the title page someone had handwritten the words, "Help me, Lord. . . . PLEASE!!!"

Crystal laid the book down and thought about the words and who might have written them. It could have been some man who was an alcoholic. Or maybe a girl who was in trouble. Maybe it was someone who was being followed by some evil person. Or, perhaps, it was someone who had just lost a loved one and was grieving. It could have been some teenager that was really depressed about grades . . . or her folks' divorce . . . or even a boyfriend.

Crystal scrunched down on the pillow and closed her eyes. She thought about how lots of people walked around with deep hurts, but everyone thought they were okay. Then all of a sudden they reacted to the hurts inside and everyone was surprised. She thought about Gabrielle. *All the kids think that good old Gabrielle is the happy Indian girl with the firey eyes and a quick smile. But inside . . . inside."* Crystal thought she was only beginning to sense some of the struggle that was Gabrielle's.

She was getting sleepy and reached over to turn off the light by the bed. *I suppose even Teresa has a hidden life. But it's a cinch she won't let anybody know about it.*

"Lil' Flash! Hey, Crys! Wake up. Get your jams on."

Crystal struggled to let the light of the motel room and the light of reason have their impact on her brain. "Huh? What?" she mumbled, sitting straight up in bed, but feeling very groggy.

Gabrielle stood next to her. "Why didn't you come on down to the pool?"

"What?" Crystal rubbed her eyes and looked around. Teresa was sound asleep under the covers in the adjoining bed. "I was waiting for Teresa. . . . I guess I fell asleep."

"Well, there she is." Gabrielle pointed. "She must have come in after you konked out. At least she got ready for bed."

"What time is it? Late, huh?" Crystal mumbled.

"It's 11:30. I guess it is kind of late. We were watching the boys show off. Shawn and Travis got into this diving contest with a couple of guys from Browning. They were all really good. Have you ever seen Shawn dive?"

Crystal got up and staggered toward the bathroom. "Dive? Well, no . . . I don't think so. I mean, I've never even seen him in a bathing suit." She muttered as she searched through her suitcase for her pajamas.

"Hey, you know who's a good diver? Travis. Really." Dusty entered into the conversation. "He did a backward flip and dive that made even the guys from Browning applaud."

"Yeah, and he almost landed on me," laughed Gabrielle. "I've got guys falling for me all over the place."

Crystal brushed her teeth, tried to comb her hair, pulled on her pajamas, and stuck her tongue out at herself in the mirror.

"Why were you waiting up for Teresa?" Gabrielle asked.

"Oh, well . . . I'll talk about it tomorrow. I'm crashing. Set an alarm, OK?" Crystal flopped down on the bed and reached for the covers.

A piercing ring jabbed through Crystal's ears and propelled her out of a dream about being stuck in a snowbank. She jumped out of bed and rammed into the wall.

"It's the phone," Gabrielle blurted. "Crystal, get the phone."

Crystal lifted the black, cold receiver and rasped, "Yeah?"

A metallic monotone responded, "Wake-up call as you requested, good morning."

"Who was it?" Gabrielle asked.

"A computer. It was for you." Crystal laughed.

"Oh, the wake-up call. Wow! It's five o'clock already. Come on, breakfast is at six." Gabrielle hustled out of bed, leaving Crystal standing in the middle of the room. "I'll grab a shower. You wake up Teresa and Dusty."

"Teresa's gone."

Crystal was starting to think a little more clearly. "Dusty, time to get up. Where's Teresa?"

Dusty brushed back her short, wavy, red hair and leaned over on her side. "She said something about early practice. I think she and her mom were going out to the arena."

"You're kidding." Crystal began to remember the discovery of the cards and red pen in the suitcase the night before. She walked over to Teresa's suitcase and glanced in it to see if she could find the evidence still there. She looked next to the bathing suits, but the cards and pen were missing.

"She's up to it again." Crystal took a deep breath and let out a sigh.

"Up to what?" Dusty came over to Crystal.

"Oh, I was just thinking about Teresa. She sure is pushing herself. Does she really enjoy all this?"

"Only when she wins," Dusty smiled. "Only when she wins."

73

Crystal was still troubled about how to confront Teresa and didn't say much as the girls got ready to go. They wore their new rodeo outfits that had been purchased for them by the Snake River Lumber Company some weeks before. She thought about pinning her hair up under her hat, but decided just to let it fall down.

"I've decided to impress them all with my great riding ability rather than my incredible good looks," Crystal told the others as she pulled on her boots and jammed her hat on her head.

"There's cutting and roping today. Barrels and poles tomorrow," said Gabrielle. "I hope I win some silver. You know, I've been so busy with school, and these notes and stuff, I haven't given a lot of thought to the rodeo. It's time to get serious."

"Gabrielle, you've got to really push. You could get the All Around buckle again." Crystal counseled like a cheerleader.

"Yeah, I want it. Especially, I want to show those Blackfeet a thing or two. But listen, it's not everything. I mean, life's more than just riding in a rodeo, right?"

"Gabrielle, you shouldn't talk that way. I mean, you've got to psyche up for the competition and . . .

"Whoa! Hey, is this Lil' Flash? Since when did you become obsessed with winning?"

"Oh, it's just that I didn't want . . . I mean, I want us all to do our very best, that's all."

"Well, I'll agree with you there. I don't plan on losing at anything."

Crystal's legs began to quiver when they pulled into the arena and headed for the barns. Looking at all the other kids arriving reminded her that she would be competing against more contestants than ever before.

"The more there are, the faster the times will be," she sighed.

She didn't spot Teresa anywhere. She and Gabrielle went to the stalls where the horses were and started getting them ready to ride. It was a quiet time, each girl carefully grooming her horse.

Caleb seemed anxious to get out. It had been three days since Crystal had given him a good workout, and she could tell he did not want to wait much longer.

The arena kept out the snow and some of the cold. But Crystal shivered in the chill of the winter air, even inside.

"I think all that riding in the travel home yesterday made me stiff," she called out to Gabrielle.

"Well, you should have gone swimming," Gabrielle chided. "Hey, look at the crowd already coming in. This is going to be fun."

"Fun? I'm getting sick at my stomach. I'm glad cutting is today. Maybe I'll be ready for barrels by tomorrow."

Crystal felt right at home in the cutting event,

and Caleb was in rare form. The big, gray Appaloosa thrived on chasing calves. *Just like dogs chase cats*, Crystal thought.

She looked up to see Teresa riding through an imaginary barrel pattern. Crystal could see the strain of concentration on Teresa's face.

"She doesn't really ever let up, does she?" Crystal motioned to Gabrielle.

"Teresa?"

"Yeah."

"No, I don't guess she does. I mean, even when she's having fun, it always seems to be for a purpose. She's got her own set of reasons for every move. But maybe that's what it takes to be the best at something," Gabrielle finished thoughtfully.

"I suppose, but is it worth the price?" Crystal wondered aloud.

"Yeah, we all have our goals in life," Gabrielle trotted her horse awhile.

"Gabrielle, what are your life goals?"

"I knew as soon as I mentioned that you would pin me with it. Crystal, sometimes you are just like Teresa. I don't have any life goals. Do you?" Gabrielle shot back.

"Oh, I guess not. I mean, I dream a lot about the future, but I'm not sure any of them are goals that I'm working to achieve. Oh, I do have one goal. Someday I want to, just once, beat both you and Teresa in barrel racing."

"Now, that is a life goal!" Gabrielle laughed.

"Hey . . . you watch me tomorrow. I want to be up there."

"Well, I can tell you one thing, Lil' Flash. You'd win the most-improved-since-September category . . . that is, if they had one. You're really getting better."

The announcer cleared the arena, and the different schools got ready to enter. The new outfits of the Highland High Team were as impressive as any. Crystal and Gabrielle used their new Snake River Lumber Company saddles for the Grand Entry.

"Look, are those real buckskin coats?" Crystal spoke to Gabrielle.

"Yeah, that's Browning for you. Probably all elk hide, if the truth were known."

Crystal's team was the third to enter the arena. The girls rode in first, four at a time. Then came the guys. By the time they circled by the grandstands, the seats were half filled with more people streaming in.

"Where's Teresa?" Crystal asked Gabrielle while still waving to the crowd.

"She's in the honor guard. She'll come in later."

"How did she get that position?" Crystal asked.

"She owns the flag."

"Really?"

"Nah, she was out here early and got in on the practice, that's all. It's no big, really."

The Highland High rodeo team waited in position, just right of center, while the other teams entered. After all the teams were in the arena, an honor guard entered carrying an American flag and a Montana state flag and an Idaho state flag. Teresa carried the Idaho flag.

"Look at her. You'd think they were competing in flag carrying," Crystal whispered.

"Listen, her points are just as welcome as anyone else's," Gabrielle cautioned.

When the Grand Entry ceremony ended they rode out of the arena and back to the barns. Gabrielle and Crystal changed saddles. As they cinched down their older, working saddles, Crystal thought of how little she and Shawn had talked lately.

They walked back out to the arena fence to watch the first event. Dust was starting to fog up the walkway between the barns and the gate next to the chutes. At that moment Shawn appeared right in front of her.

"Well, Crys, what do you think? You going to take 'em today?" Shawn asked.

"Good Lord willin' and Caleb stays healthy," she joked. "I think we ought to do all right. Don't you?"

"You'll be up there. Browning will be your toughest opponents in cutting. Now when it comes to barrels and poles, it will be Kalispell. Some of those gals can really ride."

"You've been checking them out?"

"Yeah. Strictly business. You know, trying to get a reading of the opposition." He grinned. "Hey, I'm headed for the chutes. Wish me luck. I'm riding saddle broncs first up."

"Don't hurt yourself, cowboy," she called. Shawn pushed his brown cowboy hat back and slightly bowed, then headed to the chutes.

Gabrielle tried to tackle her from behind. "Hey, have you heard from your . . . you know, friend, today?" Crystal inquired.

"Yeah, look at this last one. It was down in the barn on my tack," Gabrielle crowed.

"Uh, is it in red ink? You know, like the last one?"

"No, it's sort of early American pencil. Look, it says, 'tomorrow . . . wearing silver . . . you'll be the reason I win.' "

"Sounds like he'll be known by the end of the rodeo."

Gabrielle looked out at the riding chutes, "Yeah, and I hope I'm not disappointed."

Crystal turned her head and prayed. "Lord, please don't let Gabrielle be disappointed," she pleaded.

Crystal loved to watch the riding events, but was always fearful that someone would get hurt. The first two guys out lasted only a kick or two and then went flying to the ground.

"Are they going to have more than one go round?" she asked Gabrielle.

"Oh, sure. I think they get two rides, then the

best eight averages get a shot at the finals. You know, the fourth round is averaged in for overall winner."

The loudspeaker announced Shawn. The gate crashed open and a wild-looking, black horse flailed out. He kicked his back feet almost straight above his shoulders, then twisted right, then back left, and once more flew in the air.

Shawn looked like a limp rag doll being tossed about, but somehow he hung on until the buzzer. The pickup man pulled alongside, and Shawn grabbed hold of the man's shoulder just as the bronc decided on one more kick. The impact flipped Shawn over the top of the pickup man and into the arena dirt. He got up slowly and shuffled back to where the girls waited.

They strained to hear the announcer.

"Hey, a sixty-three—that's not bad for a roper," Shawn cheered hoarsely.

"You OK?" Crystal prodded.

"Sure, a little dirt like that keeps you humble."

The morning yielded one exhilerating ride after another. After the saddle broncs came the bareback. Shawn qualified for the afternoon finals in the saddle broncs. Several of the Highland High team scored high.

They ran the cutting event right before lunch. There were fewer entries than in most of the other events.

Shawn charged over from the chutes. "Hey,

you're on. They're going to run two short rounds; then a final this afternoon. Go get 'em."

Crystal hardly heard Shawn's words. She mentally picked over the cattle they brought in. She wanted the toughest one out there.

Almost by rote, she rode to the center arena, headed for the herd, pushed Caleb toward a flighty white face, and turned Caleb loose on him. As always with this event Caleb was ready. He snorted, stomped, and bluffed the little guy right out to the middle of the arena. The calf twisted, turned, bawled, tripped, ran, and stopped. Caleb didn't relent an inch. The crowd roared when it was over.

"Hey, I didn't know Teresa was entered in cutting," Crystal said, startled, as she and Gabrielle watched the rest from the rail.

"Well, the more events, the more points, you know."

Teresa had a good run. Crystal was only one point ahead of a girl named Cindy from Browning. Teresa was in a very respectable fifth place.

Everyone was expected to grab some lunch on their own, so Shawn and Crystal headed for the barbecue pits while the breakaway roping got started.

When they came back they noticed Gabrielle and a girl from Eureka were leading the pack. Teresa had done well in breakaway, also. She was in eighth place.

It was almost three before they were ready for

the finals. Gabrielle reported the event posting. "It's going to be girls' cutting, boys' cutting, breakaway roping, steer wrestling, bareback, and the saddle bronc," she stated to the team. "Lil' Flash, you can be our first winner."

Crystal looked everywhere for Teresa. She finally discovered her by herself on top of a pile of hay, cradling her head in her arms. She walked over that way and paused, "Hey, Teresa, you qualified in both events, right?"

"Yeah. I wish I had your Caleb in the cutting. I need a new horse. Mine are all fast and dumb," she pouted.

"Teresa, can we talk a minute? I waited up for you last night, but I guess I fell asleep."

"Listen, Crystal . . . I need some time alone right now. I've got to prepare myself for this cutting. I'll be lucky to place . . . and if I don't place here, there's no Girl's All Around silver. You know what I mean?"

"Oh, uh, sure. But this is important. Can we talk tonight?"

"Yeah, later." Teresa's eyes pierced a hole somewhere out in the arena.

Reluctantly, Crystal returned to Gabrielle and Dusty. "Boy, she's in a trance." Crystal nodded at Teresa.

"You're third up, Lil' Flash. Make it another good one."

A fresh herd was brought in for the cutting finals, and Crystal once again scanned the lot for a feisty one. She talked over her decision with Caleb. "I say we go for another white face. They seem like they just came off the range or something. You ready to go to work?"

Caleb plunged into the herd with as much enthusiasm as ever. He almost pranced over to the prey and once again started his bluffing routine. Always one or two steps ahead of the steer, he succeeded in cutting him out of the herd and out into the center of the arena. He wouldn't even let the steer break for the side rail, but insisted that he stay out in the middle. It wasn't until the announcer called time that Crystal realized the crowd was cheering.

When she got back outside the arena, Gabrielle ran up and gave her a hug. "You two did it, Lil' Flash. You'll take first place for sure."

Shawn and Travis walked up and congratulated her as well. "Hey, did you guys know that Trav qualified in bareback, saddles, and steer wrestling?" Shawn announced.

"Wow, that's great," Gabrielle shot back. "I didn't know you were a steer wrestler, Travis."

"Lots of things about this old boy you don't know," Shawn boasted, as Travis blushed.

They all leaned up against the rail to watch Teresa go through her run. She was pushing out a red Hereford that would run two feet, then stop and bawl, run two feet, then stop and bawl. She kept pushing him out to the center.

"That's not the prettiest run of the day."

Shawn announced, "But it looks like the most determined."

The high score that Teresa received showed that the judges agreed with Shawn. Crystal won the event by six points, but Teresa's last run brought her up in the average to finish third. Travis stunned the field with a great throw in steer wrestling and took first.

In the boys' cutting, none of the Highland team made the finals. In the bareback, Leon barely made it out of the chute. But Travis hung on until the buzzer, pulling down fourth place. By the time of saddle-bronc finals, Crystal's eyes blurred. It was the longest rodeo day she'd ever endured.

"Man, it seems like a year ago since morning," she told Gabrielle. "Where's Teresa?"

"She's in the barn practicing roping," Gabrielle replied. "I think she's made out of 100 percent adrenalin today. Shawn's up last. I think he can win if he gets a good ride."

"Yeah, and did you see Trav? He was clear over the top but held on. He ought to get fourth or fifth, right?" Crystal asked.

Gabrielle didn't answer, or if she did, Crystal didn't hear because the gate thundered open, and Shawn rode out on a twisting, sorrel bronc. Crystal held her breath as it kicked and slung itself sideways.

Finally, in what seemed to Crystal a lot more than eight seconds, the buzzer sounded. Shawn reached over for the pickup man. The bronc jumped into the accompanying horse causing Shawn to slip to the ground between the horses. He jerked to his knees and suddenly the bronc shot a hoof out, catching Shawn in the shoulder. The thud could be heard across the arena.

The sight paralyzed Crystal right where she stood.

She didn't scream.

She didn't move.

She hardly breathed.

6
THE REVELATION

SHAWN FELL FORWARD IN THE DIRT AND ROLLED away from the kicking horse. Travis, Leon, and several others immediately ran to his rescue, chasing off the bronc to protect him.

Gabrielle slipped her arm around Crystal; they watched intently as Shawn staggered to his feet. He flung his left arm around Travis's shoulders and hobbled toward the gate.

His right arm and shoulder slumped horribly lower than the left. Crystal could read the pain in his eyes as he approached. She wanted to hug him, but didn't dare. She wanted to say something, but didn't know what. She wanted to do something, but couldn't think of anything that would help.

"Just wait here; I'll get the doc," Mr. Duffy, the team coach, ordered as he sprinted for the stands.

Shawn gasped in a pinched voice, "It's . . . just . . . a shoulder separation. . . . Look . . . Trav . . . I need a little help." He lifted the sagging arm and bent it with the elbow pointing straight out from his shoulder.

"Now," he continued, "brace your left arm under my armpit, then take your right hand and yank straight down on the end of my elbow."

Travis backed away.

"Look, it's happened before. . . . I just popped the shoulder out. How about it?"

"Maybe we should wait for the doc, Shawn," Travis hesitated.

Shawn searched the group for someone to help. His eyes met Crystal's. Tears were starting to trickle out the corners of her eyes. She could barely manage to shake her head "no." Sheer panic took hold of her tongue and limbs.

"I'll do it." Teresa climbed over the fence and leaped down beside the guys on the inside of the arena. "I've done it for Dad a couple times."

Before Crystal knew what was happening, Teresa had a hold on Shawn. "Hang on, cowboy," she said like a Marine Corps nurse.

Shawn gritted his teeth as Teresa yanked down on the extended elbow. Crystal heard a dull pop, and the once limp shoulder now looked straight in place. But suddenly, all Crystal could see was black, empty space and hear the sound of faraway voices.

"She's fine. She just fainted."

"I'd like to go with her; I'm her friend."

"Plenty of room. Come on."

"We'll need to x-ray the boy, just in case."

"Bring them back to the motel. You've got the parental consent forms. If you need anything else, call me first."

Crystal blinked her eyes hard and tried to

focus them. An occasional light flashed by. They were moving. She was in a car. In the backseat. A man and woman sat in the front. Mrs. Patterson and someone she didn't recognize.

She slowly craned her neck. Gabrielle perched on her left, Shawn at her right.

"Hey, welcome back. You had a little snooze," Shawn said gently.

"Oh, no, don't tell me I . . ." she wailed.

"You sure did," Shawn replied. "And it would have been flat on your face, and maybe your sprained wrist, if it wasn't for Gabrielle looking out for you."

"Me and about the whole Highland High rodeo team. There's no way you were going to touch the ground with that gang crowded around," Gabrielle declared.

"Are you all right?" Crystal asked Shawn.

"Sure, ask the doc." He pointed to the man driving the car.

"Probably just the dislocated shoulder," the doctor summarized. "But we want to get some X rays and check for cracked ribs. How are you doing, young lady?"

"Oh, I feel fine, I guess. But I feel very dumb about passing out like that."

"Probably just a little too much empathy. Your body tells you it's had enough, time to release the tension. Is that the first time you've fainted?" he added.

"Yeah, and I hope it's the last." She turned to

Gabrielle, "Thanks for the help."

"Hey, Lil' Flash . . . no sweat. That's what friends are for. Here's your hat."

"Yeah, some friends faint, some jump in and help. I was impressed with Teresa. Mrs. Patterson, she sure acted like she knew what she was doing."

Mrs. Patterson twisted around. "Well, Teresa's been watching cowboys get hurt at rodeos since she could toddle around a corral. Nothing fazes her. I keep thinking she should be a vet. She seems to work best under pressure."

"I don't even move under pressure," Crystal moaned.

"I wouldn't worry about it," Mrs. Patterson smiled kindly. "You had a graceful faint."

Gabrielle laughed. "Yeah, just like a sack of potatoes falling out of the back of a truck."

"Shawn, you said this happened to you before?" Crystal prompted.

"Uh, well, let's see. Once at Jerome, once at Dillon, and last time at Horseshoe Bend. That makes four times. Anyway, with my right arm this stiff and sore, I won't be able to rope well for about three weeks. And I'll have to stay off the rough stock for a month to six weeks, right, Doc?"

The man in the gray Stetson laughed, "You've got the treatment memorized. But tell me, do you ever follow that advice?"

"Sure. This time. We don't have a rodeo for

over two months. I'll take it easy. But it sure finished my competition up here."

"The rodeo! I forgot. How did we do?"

"It was pretty good, really. I suppose we're in first place, if there is such a thing after only half the events." Gabrielle spoke up. "Shawn won the saddle bronc."

"Yeah," Shawn added, "and Gabrielle and Teresa have a good shot at All Around, if they get some good rides in tomorrow. Hey, you know who had a good day? Travis. He won the steer wrestling, and if he can do something tomorrow, who knows, he could win the silver."

After a brief trip to the hospital, they were quickly returned to the motel.

"I'm starved," Shawn exclaimed, as they hurried toward their rooms.

"Let's meet at the coffee shop in a half hour," Gabrielle suggested, as she rummaged in her purse for their key.

In the room, Dusty and Teresa were sprawled out on the beds with strawberry sodas and corn chips. Teresa sat right up. "What's the verdict on Shawn?"

"He'll be out of competition for a few weeks," Crystal reported.

"Does that mean no more ladies fainting over him?" Teresa gibed.

A crimson flush hit Crystal's cheeks. "I guess so. Really, I've never done that before. How about you?"

"Nah, but I've thought about it." Teresa strutted around the room. "See, in case this handsome hunk ever walks by, I'll bat my eyelashes and say, 'Oh, dear me,' as I crumple in his arms." Teresa swooned on the bed.

The girls howled with laughter.

"Hey, Lil' Flash," Teresa called from the bed. "Did you want to talk to me about something?"

Crystal suddenly recalled her anger of the night before, yet with Dusty and Gabrielle there all she could do was avoid the subject. "Uh, yeah, well, nothing big. Anyway, I'm hungry. Let's get ready to go eat."

For the next twenty minutes the four girls hardly spoke as they tore through the room, dressing and fighting for mirror space. Teresa flew down to her mom's room to borrow another blow dryer. Finally, with one last inspection they filed out the door.

"Uh, oh, secret admirer time," Dusty called out as she pulled a card down from under the motel room numbers. "I believe this belongs to you." She waved it in Gabrielle's direction.

Gabrielle tossed the envelope in her purse.

"What? Aren't you going to read it?" Dusty asked.

"Well, sure. Later. I mean, I wouldn't want to bore you with my mail."

"Your secret admirer is boring?" Dusty baited.

Just then several team members joined them.

"Let me see the envelope," Crystal whispered as she and Gabrielle dropped behind the others.

Crystal noted the red ink scrawls, and the size—about the same as the cards she discovered in Teresa's suitcase.

"Open it," she encouraged.

Gabrielle slid out the card. Crystal wasn't sure if it was one she'd seen the night before or not. It read, "In twenty-four hours, the masquerade will be over. See you then."

"Twenty-four hours?" Crystal repeated.

"The end of the rodeo. When the rodeo's over, then I'll know. Hey, how about our trying to figure a way for them to call off the rest of the rodeo? Then I could find out tonight!"·

Crystal whirled around in shock. "Gabrielle, you can't possibly mean that. You can't even joke about something like that. We've got to keep all our attention on our training and our purpose." She stopped, self-conscious at her outburst. "Our roles seemed to be reversed all of a sudden. Funny, huh? Anyway, you've got to go out there and do your good stuff tomorrow. You don't think your secret pal's looking for some second-rate cowgirl, do you?" Crystal prodded best she could.

A group from the Highland High team already circled a large table in the coffee shop. Shawn sat between Travis and Teresa.

"Oh, did I get your place, Lil' Flash?" Teresa asked. "I was just checking on my patient. Here, you can have him. I like mine healthy."

Several of the boys pulled up some extra chairs, and they all crowded around the table. "Gabrielle," the normally shy Travis spoke up. "Uh, listen. With Shawn out tomorrow, would you be willing to team rope with me? I've got to score some more points to stay in the running, and I can't break up one of the other teams."

"Do you really think I can do it?"

"Hey, I've watched you rope. I know you can. Do you want to head or heel?" Travis offered.

"I'd much rather heel; the back feet are easier for me. Trying to rope the head makes me nervous. That is, if that's all right with you. Can we get in some practice tomorrow?"

"You got it. Thanks."

"Hey," Crystal whispered, "I haven't heard Travis talk that much since I met him."

"Well," Gabrielle laughed under her breath, "I just have a way with guys. You know, secret admirers, guys asking me to rope. What's a girl to do?"

"Order dinner," Crystal retorted. "You're getting to sound like Teresa."

Gabrielle shot her a warning glance.

That evening Crystal relived every event and ride of the day and reviewed the next day's schedule. She still wanted to talk to Teresa, but there was never a time they were alone. *Somehow*, Crystal thought, *it's like she's avoiding me on purpose.*

In a way, Crystal was secretly relieved, because she didn't know how to confront Teresa. And if she finally knew the truth, she had no idea how to break it to Gabrielle. And if the whole business blew up before tomorrow's competition, it could penalize the whole team's chances at the rodeo.

Unless, unless, an exciting thought rushed through Crystal's mind like a thunderbolt. *I just might have the answer how to teach Teresa a lesson and at the same time avoid several unpleasant scenes.*

If I could just beat Teresa in the barrels or poles, then maybe. . . . She went to sleep reviewing all that Gretchen had told her about using the spurs.

Crystal shot up from the pillow. She heard the shower running, but could see no one in the room. When the redheaded Dusty bounced out of the bathroom drying her hair, Crystal checked on the whereabouts of the others.

"Where's Teresa?"

"Oh, you know, back out there sweating in the arena."

"And Gabrielle?"

"She left with Teresa. I think she wanted to practice roping."

I've got some practice of my own to do, she plotted silently, as she bolted from the bed covers.

When she reached the barns, she took extra time prepping Caleb. He seemed raring to go, but she knew he would be disappointed when he arrived at the arena and there were no calves to corral. Today their attention would be on barrels and poles.

Once again the schedule showed that the preliminary rounds would be in the morning, and the finals in the late afternoon. As the morning wore on, everyone began to show the strain of the intense, two-day competition.

The pole bending proved a disaster as far as Crystal was concerned. She couldn't seem to budge Caleb past a steady gallop. An exasperated Crystal was happy just to get the first ride over. The second go round was not much better. She failed to qualify for the finals, but both Teresa and Gabrielle finished in the top five.

Travis and Gabrielle won entry into the team roping finals. Then, Travis made it into calf roping, but no Highland Highers qualified for the goat-tying event.

Bull riding frightened Crystal more than any other aspect of rodeo. She was secretly happy Shawn could not enter. He hung around the chutes and helped the others instead. The entire grandstands held their breath when Leon caught his hand in the rigging, but it turned out that he was not seriously hurt.

Crystal paced Caleb in figure eight formations out in the barn area when Gabrielle and Dusty rode up. "They're dragging the arena floor for the barrels," they announced.

They got there just in time to watch the last barrel put in its place. "How many girls have entered?" Crystal asked.

"Forty, but only eight can make it to the finals." Gabrielle added, "Think you can do it, Lil' Flash?"

"I hope so. I mean, I am going to do it," she said with rare resolution.

"That's the way. Hey, look at this note I just found back in the barn." Gabrielle handed it to Crystal.

She unfolded the torn, brown paper grocery sack and read aloud,

"After the rodeo tonight,
  everything will be all right,
    the silver buckle will shine,
      and your hand will lock in mine,
        after the rodeo . . . tonight."

Crystal slammed it shut. "Meanwhile, Gabrielle Northstar, you've got a barrel race to run."

"Oh, yeah," Gabrielle commented, "kind of hard to concentrate; you know what I mean?"

Crystal just sighed.

"Teresa Patterson," Crystal muttered to herself, "I'm not going to let you do this. I'm going to outrun you if I have to pick up Caleb and carry him around the course."

Teresa and Gabrielle both had exceptional

runs in the preliminaries. Crystal's first run was good, but it was her second one that raised her hopes. Gabrielle shouted the news from the rail while Crystal chased after her hat as usual. "You're in, Lil' Flash!" You made it to the finals!"

Teresa brought them the list of the elite group of eight.

"Sherry Bartlett from Kalispell is in first. Gabrielle and I are tied, one-tenth of a second behind her. Really, all eight are pretty bunched up. You're seventh, Crystal. Congratulations!" Teresa commented.

Crystal knew it would be almost two hours before the barrel racing finals were run, but she took Caleb back to the barn area and began to regroom him. Even with the encouraging early runs, she knew it would take one incredible race to nudge Teresa out of her All Around points.

Shawn stopped by with a couple of hot dogs and some chips, but she didn't talk to him very long. However, she did do plenty of talking to Caleb.

"See, here's the thing," she spoke earnestly to the nonchalant-looking horse. "We can't let Teresa play these kinds of tricks on people like Gabrielle. So you and I need to really pour it on with this final race. Do this one favor for me, and I'll really make it worth your while. You'll get some time off. You know, a little Christmas break. Christmas! Oh, no! I still haven't got a present for Gabrielle or Shawn! I haven't even got a . . ."

"Talkin' to your horse, Lil' Flash? That's a bad sign."

Crystal spun around and nearly bumped into Teresa. "Oh, uh . . . hi."

"You working hard?"

"Yeah. I guess I'm nervous about the finals."

"I know what you mean. I have quite a chore ahead of me trying to edge out Gabrielle and Sherry Bartlett. It's awkward when the toughest competition's on your own team."

Crystal took a deep breath. "That reminds me, Teresa." She had every intention of confronting Teresa right there, but she saw Shawn advancing quickly towards them. "I, uh . . . I've got a secret weapon today," she ad-libbed.

Teresa leaned back in surprise. "Oh, yeah? What a coincidence. So do I."

Shawn interrupted further conversation. "Hey, gals, it's about time for the barrels. Thought you two might be interested."

Teresa rushed off, and Crystal blurted out, "Hold on to your hat. You're going to see me beat Teresa for the first time."

"You two building a grudge?"

"Sort of. How are you feeling?"

"Fine. A little out of it. I never was a very good spectator. You should have seen Trav ride that bull. He has a good shot at winning."

Crystal and Shawn walked Caleb back out to

the arena. "It's too bad Travis's girl friend from Nezperce couldn't be here to see how well he's doing. What's her name?" Crystal commented.

"Staley. Carolyn Staley. But anyway, didn't you know? They broke up right after Thanksgiving."

"Oh, how come?" Crystal asked.

"I really don't know. Travis doesn't talk much about himself. Now, go get 'em," Shawn concluded as he jogged over to the guys sitting on the rail.

Crystal strained to see the order for the racers as several girls huddled around the post. Gabrielle was listed third, Teresa sixth, and Crystal eighth.

"How did I end up with the last ride of the whole rodeo?" Crystal wailed to Caleb.

She rode up to Gabrielle, who waited in front of the arena gate. "You ready?" Crystal called.

"I'm ready to get this over and unmask Prince Charming," Gabrielle bantered.

"Yeah, the secret weapon," Crystal moaned to herself.

Gabrielle maneuvered a picture-perfect ride. She soared more gracefully than ever. It was a 15.812, the best of the rodeo so far.

"You wearing spurs, Lil' Flash?" Gabrielle remarked as she returned to the gate.

"Yeah, a gift from Gretchen. Hey, what a great run."

"Thanks. It'll do," she smiled.

Teresa roared up to Crystal. "Well, this is it, Lil' Flash. You're not too nervous, are you?"

Crystal absently nodded at Teresa while she followed the fluid movements of Sherry Bartlett and her handsome, creamy white horse. "That's 15.75," boomed the announcer.

Crystal turned to Teresa. "That will be hard to beat."

"Don't have to," Teresa shrugged. "She needed a win here even to be considered for All Around. But all I have to do is finish second and I can nose out both her and Gabrielle."

As Teresa high-stepped into the arena, Crystal spied the long, sharp rowels on her spurs and determined never to challenge her to a kicking match.

Teresa shot off with a beautiful first turn, dirt flying everywhere. Crystal winced as she lashed her mount to the second with a perfect twirl around. Then, she whipped him on toward the last barrel. This one he cut so quick Teresa slid to the outside of the saddle, grabbed the horn with both hands, then regained control enough to kick and whip him across the finish line.

As the pair roared out of the arena, Crystal could hear Teresa complain to Hawkeye, "You're dog food, you hear me!" She careened off and paced back and forth until the speaker blared, "15.80."

"All right!" Teresa screeched. Then she squeezed the trim mane in reconciliation. "That

100

will get me second in barrels and Girls' All Around!" She marched over by Crystal and yanked off her spurs. "My secret weapon worked," she gleamed.

Crystal felt a sudden cold sweat. She knew this had to be her best ride ever. She also knew she had a tendency to lose control if Caleb turned too sharp. She suspected that she'd either blow her past record or break both their necks.

The competition and pressure was over for everyone except Crystal, and all the teams lined the railings. It was twice the crowd she'd ever raced for. Only seconds passed as she rode from the gate to the starting line, but it was a slow stretch of agony to her.

"What am I doing here?" she gulped, as the barrel run yawned out like a foreign maze before her. Then she mentally slapped herself to attention. "OK, stay alert . . . this one's for Gabrielle. . . . Heeyaaaa!"

She slammed the quirt on Caleb's rump and flew toward the course. For a split second she forgot where she was. It was just her, the barrels, and the big, gray Appy. How different from other rides where she fought to remember what to do next. This time she and Caleb melted as one into an exacting harmony. Around one barrel, then the next they glided. A streak of speed as they bended the third, and a flash toward home.

Her hat didn't fly until the last stretch, and she finally remembered the spurs. She kicked Caleb's flanks as he shot across the finish line. Then she wondered if she could stop him in time. But he veered to the right as she clutched the horn.

The crowd roared their approval at the final result: 15.71, the best run of the day.

After the noise died down, the final standings, based on averages, were given. "The winner is Sherry Bartlett of Kalispell. Second, due to that incredible run in the final round, and edging out her teammates, Crystal Blake of Highland High. Third place goes to Teresa Patterson of Highland, and fourth is Gabrielle Northstar of Highland. Congratulations to Sherry and those fine Highland riders."

"We did it!" she hugged Caleb.

"Super! Lil' Flash, that was a great run!" Gabrielle twirled her around.

"Where's Teresa?" Crystal searched around her congratulating teammates.

"Oh, probably practicing for next time," Gabrielle laughed. "Come on, let's hear the special awards and search for that lucky guy."

"Gabrielle, I need to talk to you about that," Crystal urged.

"Shhh. Wait, listen."

"The team winner is Highland High School!" the loudspeaker blasted.

"All right! We won! Did you hear that?" They

all shouted until they were hoarse.

Crystal tried to scream above the crowd, "Gabrielle it's all just a hoax!" to no avail.

"Now, for the All Around totals. It was extremely close for the girls. The winner is Sherry Bartlett of Kalispell. Right behind her, Teresa Patterson of Highland, and then Gabrielle Northstar of Highland."

"Gabrielle . . . there isn't going to be any . . ."

"And the Boys' All Around goes to Travis Norton of Highland. Sherry and Travis, come up here and get your silver, and I'm sure the crowd will want to hear a word from you two."

"Hey, Trav! OK!" Shawn shoved his grinning classmate out into the arena. "Crystal, Travis did it! How about that?"

"Gabrielle, listen—" Crystal started again.

"Travis? Good, old, boy-down-the-street Travis?" Gabrielle mumbled as she stared out into the arena.

"No, no, not Travis," Crystal insisted. "See, Teresa wanted to win so bad she . . ."

"I thought he was going with Carolyn, over at Nezperce?" Gabrielle offered.

"No, they broke up. Anyway, listen to me, Teresa—Travis! Is it Travis?" The possibility finally hit Crystal. "But I thought . . ."

"Shhh. Listen," Gabrielle signaled.

"Uh, I'm not good at talkin'," Travis drawled, "but I sort of won it, well, to impress this girl that I like. Thanks."

"Oh, no!" Crystal's heart pounded. "Is he the one?"

"Wasn't that a great speech?" Gabrielle was radiant as she rushed over with the others to congratulate Travis.

"Where's Teresa?" Crystal called again to the backs of her teammates.

7

LESS THAN HOT PURSUIT

THE ENTIRE HIGHLAND HIGH RODEO TEAM, AND their coaches and parents celebrated the team victory down at the arena gate. Except Crystal. She pushed and shoved through the milling crowd, searching for Teresa.

She pulled Caleb to the barns and quickly bedded him down. Then she scurried through the stalls looking for any sign that Teresa had been there. She could hear the approaching shouts and laughter of her teammates. "Hey, Crys," Shawn hollered. "We did it! We showed them what a strong team really looks like."

"Yeah . . . we did do pretty well, didn't we?" She smiled weakly.

"Listen, the coach from Kalispell said he hadn't seen such team potential in years. And here's the best part. Most of us are freshmen and sophomores. That means good teams in the future, too."

"Shawn, you didn't see Teresa out front, did you?"

"Uh, no. I don't think so. Course, I wasn't looking for her either." Shawn pushed back his hat and leaned a little closer. "Is something wrong?"

105

"Oh, I don't know. I mean, I think I owe Teresa an apology. I sort of jumped to some conclusions, and well, it really bothers me." Crystal could feel the tears building.

"Hey, she's probably getting all primped up for the party at the steak house. Come on, we need to get ready, too." Shawn grabbed her arm.

"I sure hope you're right. Anyway, Caleb's all taken care of." Crystal pointed to her blanketed Appaloosa. "Where's Gabrielle?"

"With Travis, I suspect. Can you beat that? I never figured him for the note-writing, romantic type," Shawn laughed.

"I think it was very sweet," Crystal added.

"I think it worked." Shawn guided her through the crowd and out into the parking lot.

The Prime Beef Family Steak House had a framed sign inside the front door that read, *maximum occupancy 176*. Crystal was glad there was nobody around to count. She figured there were at least 250 people. Not only was the Highland team there, but also the teams from Eureka, Libby, and Browning. Crystal relished listening to the stories about rodeo almost as much as rodeo itself. The stories were always more exciting, and funnier.

By cramming into a tiny booth made for two, Travis and Gabrielle and Shawn and Crystal finally were seated.

"Hey, we only got one setting of silverware," Shawn pointed out.

"We'll just have to share," Crystal said. "I get the fork."

A harried waitress served them their dinners. Crystal was hungrier than she had imagined. She hardly looked up until she was halfway through her baked potato piled with sour cream. "You know," she paused as she peered up at Travis, "I never guessed it was you. Did you really send all those notes?"

"Yep," Travis asserted as he chomped into his steak.

"But you and Gabrielle have known each other for years," Crystal prodded.

"Yep." He hardly looked up this time.

"Well, why all the waiting until now? I mean, why the secret admirer part? Were you just too bashful to walk right up and talk to her?"

"Yep."

Shawn held his hands up. "OK, Trav, enough dominating the conversation; you'll just have to let the girls get a word in."

"I guess I don't talk much, huh?" Travis grinned.

"I'm not complaining," Gabrielle added with a smile.

"Well, I meant what I said in the notes." He looked Gabrielle in the eyes.

"Hold it. Time out! Suppertime. Food. Steak. Remember? Now, don't say something that will embarrass me," Crystal interrupted.

"Don't you have an errand to run?" Gabrielle

teased. "Hey, Travis, tell us about that last bull you rode."

Travis set down his knife and fork and motioned with his hands as he talked. "Well, this old bull, Eaglehorn, gave me fits in the chute. Know what I mean? He kept leaning me against the fence, trying to pin my leg. I knew he was an outlaw by just the way he's pitching his head. So I tell myself, if you stay on this one, you'll win some silver.

"We just fly out of the gate, and he starts twisting sideways trying to hook me with a horn, all the time he's kicking his hind feet straight up for the arena lights. By now I realize that if I ever fall off this critter, I'll be dog food. So I'm grittin' my teeth and promising the Lord I'll never ever ride another bull, when I look up and see the clowns moving in, and realize that the buzzer already rang, so I turn loose and somehow come flying down on my feet. Old Nicky chases the bull off and tells me what a great ride I had. But I'm still shaking. Then I look up to see Gabrielle sitting on the rail, and I say, 'Lord, never mind about the deal.' "

Crystal felt the eyes of many others on them. She noticed several other tables around them hushed and listening as well.

Travis dove back down into his steak. "Guess I sort of got all wound up, huh?" he mumbled.

It was dessert time before the conversation picked up again.

108

"That really looks sinful," Crystal commented.

"What? This cake?" Shawn asked.

"Yeah, look at that chocolate cake with chocolate chips and chocolate frosting, covered with hot fudge sauce. There's got to be two million calories in every piece. You and Travis ought to be ashamed," Crystal scolded.

"Look, just because you and Gabrielle don't get enough exercise to work off a few calories," Shawn retorted.

"I know a couple cowboys we could chase all over Kalispell," Crystal warned.

That's when Shawn spooned a big bite of the chocolate delight in her mouth. She choked and laughed, all at the same time, then sputtered, "Hey, those kind of calories don't count. Really. He made me eat that. You're my witnesses."

Then she remembered to canvass the room again. "Are you sure you guys haven't seen Teresa?"

"Why do you want her so bad?" Gabrielle asked.

"I'm kind of embarrased to say. It's a stupid thing," she hesitated.

"Well, Lil' Flash, we've never done anything stupid," Gabrielle deadpanned. "Tell us what it looks like."

Crystal sighed, "OK. See, I was trying to figure out who Gabrielle's secret admirer was, and all the time I kept noticing how bad Teresa wanted the All Around award. I knew she would do about anything to win, and I also knew that she would have to beat Gabrielle. You know, since Gabrielle won at Pendleton."

Gabrielle gasped. "So you thought Teresa was writing me the notes?"

"Well, the thought crossed my mind that she might think it would distract you from doing your best. Anyway, the day you got the card signed in red ink, I found a red ink pen and some cards in her suitcase, when I was putting her bathing suits back. Then when she told me she had a secret weapon for winning, I just knew she was the one."

"I can understand your feeling a little guilty about jumping to conclusions, but what's the big deal about it?" Shawn asked.

"The big deal is that all Teresa needed to do was get a second in the barrels to take All Around. She knew that, and so did I. So, I went out there with only one purpose today—to get even with Teresa for playing a trick on Gabrielle."

"You had a great run," Shawn noted.

"Yeah, but it didn't make any difference. If I would have finished sixth, instead of second, our team still would have won. And Gabrielle would still be in the same place. All I did was hurt Teresa and help Sherry Bartlett. I wasn't doing it to have a great time, or for the team's sake. I did it only for revenge, and I feel rotten."

"Well, if it's that big a deal," Shawn urged, "let's go see if we can find her."

They found only Dusty at the motel room.

"Where's Teresa?" Crystal asked.

"She left a note. Said she just wanted to be alone and thought she'd sleep in the travel home tonight."

"Boy, she's really bummed out, isn't she?" Gabrielle offered.

"Yeah. That's the trouble with having to win all the time," Dusty commented. "It doesn't leave you any room for failure."

"It doesn't leave you much room for fun, either," Gabrielle added.

Crystal regretted not to be able to set the matter straight with Teresa that very night. She tossed and turned in her sleep.

Before daylight she shook Gabrielle. "Hey, wake up! Come on, let's go out to the travel home and try to cheer Teresa up. It's the least I can do."

"Huh? What?" Gabrielle grumbled.

"I want to go out and cheer up Teresa."

Gabrielle flipped over and yanked all the covers around her. "So, go to it," she mumbled.

"But I think it would be better if someone came with me, and later we'll all be hurrying around to get home. So why not do it now? We can come right back. It won't take long and . . ."

"The rodeo's over. No more early rising for me," she yawned.

"But, Gabrielle, it's sorta in a way partly your fault, too, indirectly," Crystal suggested.

Gabrielle sat up. "Good grief. Now I'm wide awake. Okay, but we'll need our parkas."

The girls quietly dressed and stole outside. "Hey, it's not so cold," Crystal observed.

"Must be another Chinook. Strange to have them so close together," Gabrielle mused.

"I thought the travel home was right out here," Crystal said as her eyes swept through the parking lot.

"Well, it was, last night. I wonder if Teresa took it out to the arena?" Gabrielle asked.

"Surely she's still not out there practicing?"

"No telling. I guess we'll have to wait until later." Gabrielle turned back toward the rooms. "These parkas are too hot. Let's go in."

"Travis's folks came over yesterday, didn't they?" Crystal asked.

"Uh, yeah, so what?"

"Well, why don't we get him and Shawn to drive us out to the stables? Travis could drive his folks' rig." Crystal started back through the parking lot. "You go tell Dusty where we're going, so no one will worry about us, and I'll get the guys. Meet you back here in a few minutes."

"This is crazy," Gabrielle protested after her.

In less than ten minutes Travis, Shawn, Gabrielle, Crystal, and Dusty piled in the car.

"I insisted on coming along," Dusty reported. "Wow, it's too hot for this wool sweater."

"We're all overdressed for the moment," Gabrielle agreed. "I still can't believe this. It's just barely breaking daylight."

"Yeah, well, thanks, you guys," Crystal stuttered, suddenly feeling very foolish. "I guess we really should go back to the motel?" she offered.

They all turned to glare at her.

The morning sky looked wild as a bucking bronc. Hours remained before the sun would fully peep over the immense Rocky Mountains, if it showed at all. Clouds swirled in ominous formations overhead.

They pulled into the arena parking lot. "There's the travel home. I knew she'd be out here," Crystal exclaimed.

"Maybe you girls better knock on the door," Shawn suggested. "We'll wait in the car."

A few moments later Crystal waved the boys out. "She's not in there," she reported. "Come on, it looks like the barn's open."

Shawn led the way into the dark barn and fumbled for a light switch. "She must be out in the arena," Dusty commented. "Hawkeye's not in here."

"No, she's not in the arena," Travis huffed and puffed behind them. "I just checked."

"Hey, you kids looking for something?" They all turned to see an elderly man with a scoop shovel shuffle their way.

"Oh, we were looking for a friend. She drove that travel home," Crystal pointed.

"That young lady's been out here every morning. Even with the rodeo over, she's still out here. Saddled up about a half hour ago. Said she was going to do a little trail riding."

"Trail riding? But we're headed home this morning," Crystal said to no one in particular.

"Well, maybe she won't be long. Soon as this Chinook passes there won't be anyone who wants to be out on a trail. Anyway, she headed east on Swan Mountain Trail. You fixin' to ride, too?"

"Maybe." Crystal paused.

"Let's go get breakfast while we wait for her," Dusty suggested. "It's kind of early to ride."

"Sure, you guys go ahead. If I rode after her right now I could catch up with her. Maybe riding back would be a good time for us to talk," Crystal decided.

"I'm going, too," Gabrielle insisted. "Something about this whole thing's beginning to bother my Indian sense."

"So am I," said the other three at the same time.

"We can't all go," Shawn said. "Dusty, why don't you go back and tell Mr. Duffy and Mrs. Patterson what we're doing. We'll be back here at the arena in an hour or two at the most."

Dusty headed back to the car, while the other four saddled their horses. In a moment, Dusty returned. "You guys want these parkas and gloves?"

114

"I don't think we'll need . . ." Crystal started.

"We'll take them," Gabrielle insisted.

"Indian sense?" Crystal asked.

"No, Girl Scout caution." Gabrielle tied her jacket to the back of her saddle. The others followed her example.

"I think I'll take these along." Shawn pulled the wooly chaps Mr. Patterson had given him out of his gear bag. "I've been wanting to have an excuse to try them out."

It wasn't until they reached the trail into the woods that Crystal remembered how hurriedly they'd thrown on their clothes for the quick jaunt out of the motel room. "Gabrielle, do I look as grubby as I feel?" she said as low as she could.

"I don't know, how grubby do you feel?" Gabrielle whispered.

"Like after all day barrel racing."

"Yeah, that's about right," Gabrielle replied. "I'm glad we brought our hats. At least we can hide our hair with them."

"Well, it's pretty easy to follow Teresa," Shawn called back. "The trail's so muddy."

Snow littered much of the ground and still draped some of the tall, shaded pines. But the warm wind quickly converted the snow into water and slush.

Crystal watched Caleb's feet slog up the muddy trail and wondered aloud, "Do horses get cold feet?"

115

"Not as bad as boys do," Gabrielle joshed.

"Gabrielle, I'm serious. Look at this stuff we're forcing them through."

"Well, if their feet are tough enough to drive a nail into, I suppose they can take cold better than we can." Gabrielle looked on up the trail, then called to the boys, "How far are we going before we turn around?"

Shawn twisted in the saddle. "You ready to quit?"

"No, but I thought it would be good to set a limit of how far we'd go," Gabrielle returned.

"Well, how about nine? If we haven't spotted her by then, that's it," Shawn suggested.

"Yeah, that's fine."

"Shawn," Crystal asked for the first time that morning, "how's your shoulder?"

"Oh, it's just stiff, that's all."

"Has anyone got anything to eat?" Gabrielle asked.

Travis reached back into his parka and brought out a plastic sack. He took a hunk of some dark object and passed it to Shawn who grabbed a piece, then dropped back to hand it to the girls.

"Jerky! You brought some jerky?" Crystal squealed in delight.

"His dad owns the meat market, remember?" Gabrielle helped herself and put the rest in her parka.

The first big obstacle came when the trail hit

the Flathead River. "I don't know, girls, the Flathead's rocky, swift, and really cold. Maybe we should turn back now," Shawn suggested.

"Did Teresa go across?" Crystal asked.

"Well, if we are following her tracks, and we don't know that for sure, then she crossed it," Shawn reported.

"Then I say we go across. It's not nine yet," Gabrielle said.

Shawn took command. "Keep your feet up on the saddle, out of the water. Let your horse go at his own rate. If anyone stumbles, or in any way gets soaked, we're going back, Chinook wind or not."

Single file they slowly waded into the water. It was not as deep as it had looked, but the spray from the white water told Crystal it was icy. She could sense Caleb's caution. A couple times a foot slipped, but the other three stayed well anchored. Finally, they made it to the other side without mishap.

"Here, take these and dry the horses off." Shawn untied his woolly chaps and tossed them to Crystal.

"Aren't we losing time?" she questioned.

"If we lose this Chinook, the water will freeze up and these horses will be in trouble," he warned.

"If we lose the Chinook, I'm going back pronto," Gabrielle insisted.

Crystal ate the last piece of jerky about 8:30.

117

She concentrated a moment on the whirling clouds that now seemed lower. "Is it starting to get colder?" she asked.

"I haven't noticed," Shawn called. "But the weather is strange. Maybe we should . . . "

"Look! Up on that mountainside. Is that a horse?" Travis pointed to the timberless incline ahead.

"Yeah, it is! That must be her. Let's hurry," Crystal cried out.

They pushed on up the trail. It was farther than they imagined. Instead of a straight line, it bent and curved with every contour of the mountain. Much of the trail hid in the shadows of tall trees.

As they climbed out of timber and onto a snow-covered rocky trail, an old man coming toward them on a mule startled them. "Time to get to the lowlands," he called. "Chinook's busting up!" He just kept riding by them.

"Hey, whoa, old-timer," Travis hailed.

"Ain't no time. Got to get across the Flathead."

"Have you seen a girl on the trail?"

"Yep," he shouted back.

"Where is she?" Crystal rode toward the retreating old man.

"About five miles up, I reckon, and a durn fool." He stopped to look back. "You coming on down?"

"We've got to go find her," Crystal explained.

"Then you're all durn fools," he exploded and kicked his mule. Then he stopped abruptly once more. "If you got to act like fools, then go on up twelve miles to the Lazy Coty cabin. Course it ain't much. I ought to know, I'm Lazy Coty.

"But don't you go dying on me up there. I don't aim to dig no graves in the spring." And he disappeared into the trees.

Crystal returned to the others. "Wow, that wasn't very encouraging."

"Depends on how you look at it," Gabrielle added. "At least we know we are on the right trail."

"Yeah, well, let's hustle. I feel the temperature dropping," Shawn called.

The quartet, now warmly coated with parkas, continued on up the bare trail.

"It's like stumbling into a big walk-in freezer after playing outside on a hot-summer day," Crystal shivered. "How cold do you think it is now?"

"Can't tell till we start to break ice," Shawn reported.

The dark clouds pressed down closer to them. Travis stopped them and pointed down at the ground. "It's freezing up already. Must be about twenty-five and dropping."

"Surely Teresa will be turning back now," Gabrielle said. "Why is she going so far?"

As they started a short descent it began to snow. It was not the quiet, gentle snow that drifted down at night and painted the front porch white by morning. Crystal had never seen it come down so hard. Soon the trail vanished.

Shawn led the way; Travis rode to his right, only a half step behind. Gabrielle followed the boys, and Crystal trailed her. The snow now whipped straight into their faces. Crystal tilted her hat forward for some protection.

After a few moments she looked up into snow so thick she could not see more than a foot or two in front of her. Gabrielle and the boys were nowhere in sight.

"Gabrielle!" she screamed.

The lonely roar of the storm was her only reply.

8

WARMING UP

SHAWN!" CRYSTAL CRIED.
She frantically scoured the blowing snow for signs of another horse. Nothing was visible. Not even trees . . . or sky . . . or ground. Even up and down were in question. She could not discern the clouds from the falling snow or where the falling snow separated from the blowing snow or where the blowing snow met the snow piled on the ground.

But Caleb kept plodding forward.

"Shawn!" It seemed like a frigid, arctic, dream world.

Crystal suddenly caught sight of a hand holding Caleb by the nose. "Oh, Shawn," she shouted in relief, "I thought I was lost!"

Shawn leaned as close as he could to her and yelled, "We all are."

Travis and Gabrielle came into view on the ground, walking their horses. The quartet huddled together.

"What do we do now?" Crystal asked.

"Well, I think we ought to keep the old blood circulating." Shawn still had to shout although his face was only a couple feet in front of Crystal's. "So we'll walk the horses from here on.

Gabrielle, do you have your rope?"

"Yeah." She reached up on the saddle to loosen it. "You think we should tie ourselves together?"

"That's what I'm thinking," Shawn yelled. "I'll tie my rope to me and Crystal. You tie yours between you and Crystal, and Travis, you tie yours between you and Gabrielle. Trav, you better bring up the rear."

"Looks like these guys are ready to tie the old knot with us," Gabrielle teased.

"Please don't, Gabrielle, it's too cold to laugh," Crystal groaned.

Shawn quieted them. "I'll just keep walking slowly down this mountain until we hit timber. Sooner or later we've got to come to better ground than this."

"What about Teresa?" Crystal called out.

"One thing at a time," Shawn replied. "All we can do now is pray for her." He turned to the others. "We'd better be praying for all of us. I mean it!"

As she trudged through the wall of biting snow, Crystal tried not to think about her freezing ears and toes. *Why is it*, she thought, *that life changes come so quickly? Two or three hours ago we were tucked in bed with nothing more important to think about than an apology. Help us, Lord, please!*

That desperate cry to God suddenly grabbed Crystal's mind. *That's what was in the Bible in the motel room! Someone who was just as desperate as I am now.*

Crystal decided they were definitely back to slow time. She brushed aside the snow on her watch to see that it had only been a few minutes since they tied themselves together. This was not the kind of adventure that she enjoyed. Some experiences were new and thrilling. Some terrified her. This was one of those.

They reached the forest. Crystal could only see one tree at a time, and then only one that was about three feet away.

Once again Shawn huddled them together. "This storm is blowing sideways. Notice how it instantly sticks to the side of the trees? Now, if it's blowing in from the north, the way most cold storms do out here, then we're headed east. That trail we were on was going east, so I'm going to keep us going that direction." Shawn pointed and waved his arm as he yelled out. "Anyone got a better idea?"

They all shook their heads.

"Then shorten the ropes up. We could get tangled in trees or something. Keep a lookout for Teresa or the old man's cabin. We've got to get out of this storm soon." He turned and led on.

As she wandered through the storm, Crystal got to thinking about something she had read about in a sixth-grade history book. *The Donners. They were a family or caravan that went through snow like this. Did they all die? No, no, someone lived to write about it.*

She desperately tried to think about something else.

Crystal began to wonder what frostbite felt like. Her hands, even with snow gloves, felt numb. So did her ears, her nose, and her cheeks. She reached up and brushed some snow off Caleb's head and face. He was walking slowly now. Every step was careful, deliberate.

Crystal ached for a rest. She'd dearly have loved to lie down and sleep anywhere. But six inches of powdered flakes now covered whatever old snow had been underneath. Sometimes they plowed through drifts as deep as Crystal's waist.

The trees of the forest, rather than provide some shelter, made the surroundings darker and the travel harsher. Several times the safety ropes got tangled and caught in branches and bushes along the way.

This time it was Gabrielle who huddled them up. "Look! The trees now have snow blown on them from all sides. How do we know we're not going in circles?"

"We don't," shouted Shawn. "But what choice do we have?"

"We could take a nap. I'm so sleepy," Crystal complained.

"Yeah, it's our bodies slowing down. That's why we have to keep walking." Shawn turned to head on out.

Suddenly they hit heavy brush and timber on

124

the ground. It was difficult to keep finding a path to lead the horses through. The ropes got caught on snags, and there was constant backtracking to untangle and search for a new passageway.

"Look, some of this timber has been logged out," Shawn shouted as he pointed to a stump which Crystal could barely detect in the blizzard. "It means there might be a road or trail out of here. Keep looking for anything unusual!"

Crystal plodded on, wondering how they were going to find anything unusual when she couldn't even see Gabrielle behind her or Shawn ahead of her. She only knew they were there by the constant tug of the rope.

"Hey! Look!" It was Gabrielle who pulled on the ropes and was shouting to be heard. "What's that?"

"Is it a stove?" Crystal perceived something ahead of them that looked like a smokestack about ten feet high. Travis climbed up on the side of it and brushed away the snow to reveal some rusted metal. "It's a donkey engine. An old donkey engine!" he reported.

"A what?" Crystal called.

"An old steam engine used in pulling out logs," Shawn called.

"Will it help us?" Crystal yelled.

"No," he hollered. "But does anyone have a match? There might be enough protection beside it to build a fire and warm up."

They searched through the pockets of their parkas. "Hey, hey!" Crystal called.

"You got matches?" Gabrielle swept snow back from her face.

"No, look! Four pieces of hard peppermint candy. From the steak house," Crystal told them.

"All right!" Shawn cheered.

With numb fingers all four carefully removed the wrappers and pushed the candy past frozen lips into cold, dry mouths.

"I'm going to try following a straight line downhill from this donkey engine. Maybe there's a skid row down there." Shawn turned in that direction.

Crystal marveled at how four pieces of hard candy suddenly cheered them so much. The night before, when she had crammed them into her pocket, she thought nothing of it, mere trifles after the big meal at the steak house.

She figured that Shawn must have been right about a skid row. Although they still could not see more than a couple feet, no more logs and branches tripped them. Crystal began to doze off and on while still traipsing ahead.

Caleb's snort and whinny startled her eyes back open. "What is it, big guy?"

His head was tilted sideways as if to listen. Crystal pulled on the ropes. Soon the others gathered around.

"Caleb heard something. I think we've got to

126

go look. Maybe it's Teresa," she suggested.

"We can't chance losing our direction again," Shawn started.

Travis pulled in and spoke up. "I'll stay here on the trail. You guys let out the ropes as far as they will go as Shawn heads out there. If you get to the end of the ropes and still haven't seen anything, then we'd better stay on this path."

In a few moments Shawn returned through the snowstorm to announce, "The mountain seems to fall off in that direction. And there's an elk caught in the brush or something not more than thirty feet downhill. If we had a club and a match, we could have dinner. Come on, we'll be able to make it back up here."

Crystal was about five feet from the big buck before she could make out its form. It jerked wildly trying to pull its left rear hoof from out of the snow-covered ground.

Shawn yelled, "Crys, you and Gabrielle hold the horses. Trav, let's rope him and see if we can get him headed uphill. Maybe he can twist himself free, or we can pull him out."

Crystal led Caleb and Shawn's horse over a few feet and then sat down on what seemed like a pile of rocks. The elk struggled more viciously as Shawn's rope tightened around its big rack of antlers. She thought it was strange that the animal was more afraid of them than the storm.

Suddenly the big elk broke free, dragging Shawn's rope uphill with him. "Hey, come back with my rope!" Shawn howled, but Crystal could barely hear him.

"Great," Shawn rasped, "now we have one less rope."

"Come here," Travis called.

He was down on his hands and knees peering into the hole where the elk had been stuck. "This goes forever."

They all stared down into the blackness. "Put your arm in there. It's like a big den or something. I can't reach the sides or the bottom."

Shawn got down and thrust his arm into the hole. "Hand me that branch, Gabrielle." He shoved the branch all the way down into the opening.

"That's big enough to be a cave. Let's ease our way downhill and see if there's an entrance," he called.

"Look at this, you guys," Crystal yelled. "It's so cold these rocks froze together." She brushed off some of the snow from where she had been sitting.

"Froze together?" Shawn replied. "Those are cemented together!" He and Travis hurried over and scooped off more fresh snow. "There's a hole in the middle . . . like . . .

"It's a chimney!" Shawn croaked. "We're on top of a dugout!"

Gabrielle began to pace some steps. Crystal could feel the tug of the rope between them. "Maybe the entrance is over he—"

Gabrielle let out a scream and disappeared from sight. The rope pulled taut, and suddenly Crystal was flung off her feet and through the storm, over the edge of the unseen dugout roof. She plummeted into a snowbank about four feet from Gabrielle.

Both girls lay motionless a moment. Then Crystal tried to catch her breath. "Gabrielle, are you okay? If you are, say something." Crystal gingerly rolled over and tried to struggle to her feet.

Gabrielle giggled and kicked her feet, "Hey, that was fun. Do you want to do it again?"

"Look! Gabrielle, behind you! A cabin."

They almost had to stand close enough to touch it in order to tell what it was.

"It must have been dug back into the mountain," Gabrielle commented. "Help me dig out the snow in front of the door."

Just then Shawn and Travis trudged around with the horses. "We must have been on top of it," Shawn whistled as he bent to help the girls. "Looks like some kind of heavy, wooden door."

Crystal entered first, but couldn't see anything in the pitch black. Shawn and Gabrielle followed. They stumbled around a few minutes bumping into things.

"A candle!" Shawn yelled. "I think I'm holding a candle."

"Shawn, you don't have to scream anymore," Gabrielle cautioned.

"Sorry. Again we need some matches."

"We keep them on the mantel at home," Gabrielle offered. "Can you feel that rock fireplace? Maybe it has a mantel."

"I found them!" Crystal was now the one shouting. After a dozen tries she finally lit one and cautiously slid towards Shawn's flickering shadow.

The wick gradually began to blaze and lighten most of the building. The dim outlines of a cabin's interior came into view.

Shawn scooted for the door again. "You girls look for some more candles or a kerosene lamp or something. I'll help Travis pull the saddles off the horses, and we'll tie them out front."

By the time the boys brought in the last two saddles, the girls had discovered a table with a kerosene lamp. Crystal tried without success to light it.

"Here, give me the matches." Gabrielle pulled off her gloves. "This isn't a job for city girls." She smiled with near frozen cheeks.

They all laughed and hugged each other when Travis discovered a stack of firewood in the corner and a box of kindling next to it. "Hey, look at this sign above the fireplace," he said pointing.

"Lazy Coty's," Crystal hooted. "We found the old man's place!"

The fire soon roared, but Crystal was sure it would be June before she had any feeling in her toes or face. The quartet collapsed on the floor and stared at the fire for a long time without speaking.

"I was really scared out there," Crystal admitted. "I'm sure you guys are used to snowstorms, but I wasn't too sure we would make it. You know, the Donner party and all that."

"Donner party? Wasn't that the group that survived by eating . . ."

"Gabrielle!" Crystal threatened.

"Changing the subject," Shawn said as he stood up, "I am hungry. Old Lazy Coty was headed down the hill so fast surely he left some food here. And I want us to remember everything we use. We'll owe him some supplies when we get out of here."

Shawn walked over to the cupboards and began banging around. "All I can find is six cans of peaches. You guys hungry for peaches? Hey, bingo! Hot cocoa mix. Just add hot water. Now if we had some water."

"In here," Gabrielle called. "There's a water jug over here. Anyway, I think it's water. But how do we heat it?"

"Look." Travis stood up. "There's a cast-iron teakettle. It's hanging on that hook in the fireplace."

The now only half-frozen quartet hunkered down in front of the fire, each with a can of very cold peaches, while they waited for the water to boil. Crystal couldn't find four cups in the cabin. Shawn and Travis mixed their chocolate in soup bowls. No one complained.

"Old Coty must have had some meat around here," Shawn said. "In this kind of weather he probably has an outbuilding or smokehouse where he hangs the meat. He might even have a stable or barn around. Do any of you want to go out and look?"

No one volunteered.

"My ears hurt so bad I'd like to scream," Crystal reported.

"That's the way my toes feel. I don't think I could go out for a while," Gabrielle stated.

Travis piled more wood on the fire. "There's only enough wood for a couple hours. Chances are Coty has some more firewood around, also. In two hours, someone will have to go out."

After their third cups of hot chocolate, Gabrielle and Crystal leaned against each other and began to drift off to sleep. Once or twice Crystal peeked out to see Travis add another log to the fire.

Help me, Lord . . . please! Over and over the thought raced through Crystal's dozing brain. Suddenly, she sat up. Gabrielle slipped to the floor with a thud.

"Teresa! We forgot Teresa!"

"What? What?" Gabrielle murmured.

Crystal glanced over at the boys, still bundled up in parkas and gloves, cowboy hats pulled across their faces, sound asleep. "Shawn! Travis! We've got to find Teresa!"

Travis raised up on one elbow. "We've got to get some firewood. That fire's about out. What time is it?"

"One. It's one o'clock! Come on."

"Here are a couple blankets. Wrap them around you, and we'll take a look outside," Shawn instructed.

They rammed open the heavy door. The sun's brilliant reflection off the glistening, fresh snow partially blinded them. Crystal covered her eyes. "What happened to the storm?"

"Obviously, it blew over," Gabrielle pointed out. "But it didn't warm up much."

"Hey, looks like a barn." Travis motioned toward several other buildings just down the mountain slope from the little cabin. They investigated and discovered enough room for all four horses inside and some hay to feed them.

"This one has half an elk still hanging in it. We could barbecue steaks," said Shawn.

"And there's firewood. Plenty of firewood," Travis added.

"What's that building over there?" Crystal pointed.

"That, Lil' Flash," Gabrielle laughed, "is the natural bathroom."

"We've got to look for Teresa," Crystal covered. "She'll be frozen."

"Well, it looks like a trail right up the side of this canyon and past Coty's place. If Teresa stayed on the trail she either went past the house in the storm and didn't see the buildings, or she didn't make it this far. There won't be any tracks in this fresh snow, unless she's still riding."

"Maybe we should split up and look both ways," Travis suggested.

"OK. You and Gabrielle go downhill," Shawn instructed. "But stay on the trail and only go one-half hour, then turn back. We'll do the same on up the mountain. We'll meet back at the cabin around two or two thirty, right?"

Crystal and Shawn started hiking up the hill. Some places on the trail had three- and four-foot drifts.

"Shouldn't we ride the horses?" Crystal spoke as they plowed through another drift.

"They're cold and worn out, too. We need their strength to ride out of here. If we leave by three, maybe we can make it back down to a road before dark." Shawn pulled Crystal on through another drift. "At least it's so cold that the snow is fairly dry."

They walked hand in hand up the snow-covered road. To the east the huge, snow-covered wall of the Rocky Mountains towered above them.

"You know what this looks like?" Crystal asked.

"What?"

"Like one of those beautiful calendar pictures. You know, where everything is covered with snow. It's always the December picture, right?"

"Yeah, it is beautiful, isn't it?"

"We should have brought a camera."

"We shouldn't be here at all. Can you imagine what the parents and coaches are thinking?" Shawn shook his head. "Man, if my folks know, they'll be worried sick."

"Shawn, we've just got to find Teresa. I really feel responsible. You know what? I figured it out today. Teresa and I are a lot alike. Those things I don't like about Teresa are the very same things I don't like about myself. I think that's why we rub each other wrong sometimes."

"I don't think you're too much alike," Shawn rebutted as they continued to plunge up the trail.

"No, really. Inside we think a lot alike. We just show it in different ways. See, Teresa doesn't like to do anything unless she can be the best. She's trying to prove herself the top dog so everyone will treat her right. And we just promote that. I mean, we all like Teresa because she gets points for the team, right?"

"Yeah, I guess."

"Well, what if we liked her without hesitation, whether or not she was winning every race?"

"Makes sense to me," Shawn replied. "You've been thinking about this a lot, I can tell."

"It's been an emotional week. I don't know . . .

"Shawn! Across there in that opening. Look! It's Hawkeye. That's Teresa's horse!"

They left the road, climbed a snowbank, and crunched their way up a steep, snow-covered, sloping mountainside.

"What is this?" Crystal asked. "It doesn't feel the same. Are we hiking on ice?"

"Yeah, I do believe it's a glacier," Shawn informed her.

They climbed over to where the horse stood.

"Where's Teresa? Did she fall off?" Crystal inquired.

"I don't think so. She pulled off the saddle and blankets. Look over there by you. Kick that snow back."

"Shawn. It's her! She's under the saddle blanket!"

"She must have curled up on the pad and pulled that little blanket over her." He came closer. "She looks frozen."

"Shawn, is she—Shawn, I can't take it if she's . . ." The tears poured down Crystal's cheeks, freezing in place about halfway down.

He bent down, pulled off his glove, and felt for a pulse on Teresa's neck.

"She's got a heartbeat. It feels weak, but I don't know what it's supposed to feel like. We've got to get her back down to the cabin."

"You can't carry her; your shoulder's too sore."

"Yeah, and I can't lift her up on the horse. I'll go find Travis and Gabrielle. You stay here and warm her up."

"I can ride for help. Maybe you should stay here." Crystal added, "I don't know what to do."

"All you have to do is sit there on the pad, wrap that blanket around her, and hold her tight. You've got to share some of your body heat with her. Do you insist I stay to hold her?"

"I'll stay," Crystal stated.

Shawn saddled up and slowly eased Hawkeye down the hill. A moment later he was out of sight.

Meanwhile, Crystal cradled the unconscious Teresa into her arms and wrapped the blanket around both of them.

The snow sparkled like diamonds as the sun's rays danced off each frigid prism. Every tree was crowned with solid white. The unclouded sky boasted a deep, dark blue. It was absolutely quiet. The only sound Crystal heard was that of her own voice.

She rocked Teresa back and forth. "Come on, kiddo," she crooned softly, "come on, you've just got to be all right.

"Help us, Lord . . . please!"

WHAT FRIENDS ARE FOR

A s Crystal held Teresa's icy body, she gazed across the glacier. Her eyes gradually adjusted to the piercing sunlight, and she noticed a crevice in the glacier, barely ten feet away from them. It seemed to be about four feet across, but Crystal couldn't tell how deep it was. "It's a good thing she stopped where she did," Crystal shuddered.

Even though Teresa responded in no way, Crystal talked out loud to her. "Like I do with Caleb," she mused. "Teresa? Listen, I'm really sorry about my run being the one that bumped you out of the All Around award. I mean, I really didn't know I could go that fast. You know that I've never been that good before. It's just that I was feeling overprotective about Gabrielle."

She rewrapped the blanket more tightly around Teresa and looked back across the snow for some sign of the others, then continued to talk.

"When I think about it . . . I'm not much better than the others. I mean, being overprotective is about as patronizing as prejudice, I think. Anyway, I'm really sorry. You're such a good rider I didn't think I'd have a chance. But I really don't

138

think you should push Hawkeye so much. There's only so . . ."

"He won't go on," a voice rasped.

Goose bumps raced across Crystal's body. "What? Teresa! Teresa. What did you say?"

"He wouldn't go on." Her voice wasn't much more than a whisper this time. "I kept kicking him through the storm, and he just stopped, like a stubborn mule."

"Who, Hawkeye?"

"Yeah. Where's Hawkeye?"

"Shawn took him back for help."

"Crystal? Shawn? What are you guys doing up here?" Teresa opened her eyes slightly for a minute, but closed them quickly as the sun glared off the snow.

"We were looking for you." Crystal didn't let up from holding Teresa.

"Did you come through that storm?" Teresa struggled to spit out the words.

"Yeah, we came through the storm. But we found a cabin just down the road."

"Why did you come after me?"

"Why? Because you're our friend. And I felt crummy about bumping you out of . . ."

"Yeah, I heard."

"You did?"

"Yeah, it was weird. I could hear everything you said, but I couldn't talk. It was like I was paralyzed." Teresa tried to open her eyes once more. She just cracked them a little bit.

"You heard everything?" Crystal asked.

"I heard you say, 'Help us, Lord . . . please.' "

"Did you hear what I said to Shawn?"

"Uh, well, I guess I didn't hear everything. What did you say?"

"Oh, nothing. Listen, we'll get you to the cabin and warm you up pretty soon now." Crystal stared straight ahead. "What was that about your horse not going ahead?"

"I was so cold and sleepy in that storm. I was going to ride him to timber and find a place to rest. But he just balked. I couldn't budge him. I was so furious, if I'd had a gun I would have shot him."

"Teresa, you should be grateful that Hawkeye stopped when he did. Look over there; can you see that crevice in the glacier?" Crystal pointed out from under the blanket.

"Glacier? We're on a glacier?" Teresa tried to focus her eyes. "Do you think Hawkeye knew that was there?"

"I sure do." Crystal's ears pricked up. She whirled around to see the others tromping across the snow and ice. "Here they come."

"They?"

"Shawn, Gabrielle, and Travis. Hey, would you believe that it was Travis who sent her all that stuff?"

Teresa visibly seemed to come to life. "They came up here after me?"

"Hey, kiddo, you're a friend. Do you think

there's any way you can stand up?" Crystal tried to prop Teresa up, but before she could take a step she sank back into Crystal's arms.

"Not yet. I need a little more rest."

"Teresa!" Gabrielle shouted as she got closer. "Did you stay out here during that storm?"

Teresa burst out crying. "Man, am I glad to see you guys. I think this is the dumbest thing I've ever done." Then she attempted a smile. "Of course, it's the only dumb thing I've ever done."

"We'll start the true confessions later. We've got to figure a way to get you back to the cabin," Shawn began. "I'm still too bunged up to carry anyone. Trav, you'll have to try it with Teresa piggyback. Crystal, can you and Gabrielle help her up there?"

"Sure, but first come look at this, guys."

They crept up as close as they dared to the glacier opening. "That's what you call a jagged scar," Crystal gasped. "How deep would you guess it is?"

"It must be twenty feet deep," Shawn exclaimed. "You slip off in there and survive the fall, there's no way to climb out."

"Yeah," Travis added, "and if it keeps snowing, there is no way anyone would find you."

"Not until the end of the ice age," Gabrielle said in awe.

"The Lord was really looking out for you," Crystal said to Teresa as they cautiously stepped back from the edge.

They lifted Teresa to Travis's back. With Crystal and Gabrielle helping push, and Shawn leading the way, they plowed their way back to the cabin. Soon they had a roaring fire.

"Don't let Teresa get too close to the fire. She's got to thaw out a little more gradually," Gabrielle warned. "And keep her wrapped up."

Travis carried in some thin strips of meat he cut off the carcass that hung in the smokehouse. They roasted it over the fire and soon feasted on hot chocolate and elk.

"This might be the best meal I've ever had!" Crystal said as she handed some more meat to Teresa. "How you doin'?"

"My ears feel like they are going to fall off, and my toes are like wood, but my throat and stomach feel a lot better," she added.

"Trav and I are going to check on the horses," Shawn announced as he pulled on his coat. "We just sort of shoved them into the barn."

Gabrielle and Crystal huddled on both sides of Teresa.

It was Teresa who spoke up. "You know, you guys are really taking good care of me. I feel rotten about putting you through all this. It's just . . . well, I really don't know how to handle the situation when I don't reach my goals. Do you know what I mean?"

"Yeah, we can all relate to that," Crystal said, "but why do you push yourself so much? You're really good already."

142

"Well, you've seen all those trophies in our den?"

"Yeah, they're fantastic," Gabrielle replied.

"Ever since I was a little girl I've looked at those and thought that I should be adding to the collection. I love those trophies; it's sort of like a history of our family. And to add some trophies is like adding my own unique part to the history. Does that make sense? But don't get me wrong. My folks have never pushed me. It's just that I feel a failure if I go out and don't have something to show for it."

"I sort of know what you mean," Crystal broke in. "My folks write books, you know? And I always think I've got to get an A+ on all my school essays or I'm letting down the family. Is that kinda like what you feel?"

"Yeah, I guess. Then with you two on the team I feel extra pressure," Teresa continued.

"You mean me and Gabrielle?" Crystal looked at Teresa, who sat in the middle of the room, wrapped in blankets, still a little blue, her voice not very confident. It was a Teresa that Crystal was not used to seeing.

"Sure. I knew the team was fairly weak last year, especially the girls. So I've figured all year how I was going to come in and, you know, sort of turn things around single-handed. Well, things got turned around. But a lot of it's due to you two. Sometimes I envy you guys."

"You envy us?" Gabrielle asked.

"Sure. Crystal moves up here, has someone give her a horse, and suddenly in just a few months she's winning races. Then you, Gabrielle. I've never seen you have a bad run in your life. I think you're the most natural rider I've ever known. So here's good old Teresa who's been bouncing up and down on saddles since I could walk, trying to keep up. Why do you think I was out there for all those long hours in the arena? I just had to win!"

Gabrielle stared at the fire as she answered. "I think you're probably right about me. I don't practice all that much. Mainly it does come natural. But you're the winner, Teresa. You're the one the whole team wants running when we need a few last points to win. I mean, no one on earth can concentrate on winning, day in and day out, like you can."

"When you think about it," Crystal added, "it's really amazing that three freshmen girls can do as well as we did here in Kalispell. Just wait until next year—we'll finish one, two, three in everything."

"But who will be first?" Teresa asked.

"Why, me, of course!" Crystal laughed.

"No way, Lil' Flash, I'll be there," Gabrielle kidded.

"All right, you rookies. You'll have to beat me to get there." Teresa started to laugh, then stopped. "That hurts."

"Any way you slice it, finishing one, two, three

144

is a win situation, right?" Crystal challenged both girls.

"Yeah, you said it." Teresa continued, "You know something funny? I was collapsing out there in the snow, and I kept thinking, I can't go to sleep, I haven't congratulated Crystal. I kept saying, 'Where is she? Where is Crystal?' You did have one great ride, cowgirl. You want to hear something funny? I already sent cards to my sisters telling them I won."

"Did you use a red ink pen?" Crystal asked.

"Yes, why?"

Shawn burst through the door. "Hey, I think we had better move out. It's still clear, and you can see the trail down the mountain fairly well by where the trees have been logged out. But if another storm hits we'll be stranded a long time."

"Can the horses make it?" Gabrielle asked.

"Ours look pretty good, but we'll have to be careful with Hawkeye."

"Can Teresa make it?"

"Well, she'll have to ride double, but we'll probably need someone to hold onto her anyway. I think we had better get on down the mountain," Shawn urged.

"She can ride with me," Crystal volunteered. "Can we take the blankets?"

"Sure, and have Teresa wear those woolly chaps. I'm going to saddle up. You guys put the fire out with the water."

Gabrielle and Crystal scurried around to straighten up the little cabin. Finally, satisfied that everything was in order, they bundled up in parkas and gloves.

"Can you walk at all yet?" Crystal asked Teresa.

"Hey, I'm OK, just a little weak," she answered.

Crystal had Teresa mount first, then she climbed on behind. Teresa was still wrapped in blankets, and Crystal reached around her and took the reins. They headed down the hill with Shawn leading, Crystal and Teresa behind him, then Gabrielle, and finally Travis, who led Hawkeye beside his own horse.

It was so cold that Crystal could feel the frost on her lungs whenever she breathed hard. The little troop quietly forged their way along. Even though it was only a little past three, the sun was far down in the west. Crystal's cheeks and forehead burned. "How can I be sunburned and frozen at the same time?" she pondered.

"How you doin'?" she asked Teresa.

"I was thinking about moving to Hawaii," she replied. "Is it ever cold in southern California?"

"Sure. Some mornings it gets down in the forties."

A few minutes later, Shawn turned back for a discussion. "Good news and bad news. First, this is definitely the right trail. But the bad news is that over that draw is the Flathead. I'm not sure we can cross it safely again."

"We did it before," Gabrielle offered.

"Yeah, but we had a Chinook blowing, and we weren't half frozen or worse." Shawn looked right at Teresa.

"What are the options?" Crystal asked.

"Well, we could stay on this side of the river and continue downstream hoping to find a road, bridge, or crossing somewhere. Eventually we'd have to hit the Glacier National Park Highway, right?"

"Yeah, but who knows how long that will be? We don't have more than an hour's worth of daylight. We've got to chance it across that river," Travis interceded with his longest speech of the day.

"Can we make it doubled up?" Teresa asked nervously.

"I don't think so," Shawn replied.

"Listen," Crystal interrupted. "If you can hang on, you ride Caleb across, then send him back, and I'll ride him."

"Yeah," Shawn added, "I could lead him back for Crystal."

"No, that would mean you'd have to cross three times," Crystal protested. "I really think Caleb will come back on his own. Anyway, I'm willing to give it a try."

Down the draw Crystal slid off the back of Caleb and into the snow. She pulled her hat down and turned up her collar. Then she gave

Caleb his instructions. "Listen, Caleb, you've got to cross that river very carefully. Then, you've got to hightail it back across here when I holler."

Crystal waited at the edge of the frigid waters of the Flathead. The water near the bank was already starting to refreeze after the earlier Chinook. Once in a while she spied chunks of ice propelled down the white-water rapids.

She watched Shawn reach the far bank, then Gabrielle. Teresa advanced very slowly, with Travis close by.

Suddenly a noise behind her caused Crystal to spin in her tracks.

"Uh, nice doggy," she stuttered as she stared at two snarling, grayish animals about the size of huge, shaggy German shepherds. They inched a step toward her, baring their teeth. "Oh, no," she wailed. "I don't think they're dogs! They look more like—wolves!"

"Caleb! CALEB!" she screamed. The roar of the river drowned her appeal. She attempted frantically to wave at those across the river without taking her eyes off the beasts. The largest of the two began a slow circle to Crystal's left. "They're getting ready to move in," Crystal yelped in fear. "Caleb! Caleb!"

She grabbed for something to throw at the wolves. Everything was covered with snow. She started backing toward the river. "I wonder if wolves can swim? Of course they can swim;

dogs can swim. Can they swim in freezing water? Can *I* swim in freezing water?" she chattered.

The wolves growled and stalked as Crystal reached down to make a snowball to throw, but the snow was too cold and dry to stick together.

"Caleb!" she called again.

The wolves stopped to glance at the river. Then, their growling intensified. Crystal quickly stole a look back over her shoulder just as the big, gray Appaloosa pulled himself out of the river and shook himself dry. Immediately Crystal ran for the saddle. As she darted forward the wolves attacked.

She had her left hand on the horn and her left foot in the stirrup, but was not yet in the saddle when Caleb spun to lash out at the wolves with his hind feet. Crystal shot forward, clutching at Caleb's neck. She was clear out of the saddle, but managed to hang on.

Caleb twisted from side to side to kick at the wolves. He caught one in the side and flipped it about twenty feet back into a snowbank. That wolf cowered when it rose. Caleb's sudden turns and hard kicks made Crystal's ride like trying to stay on a saddle bronc, but she held tight.

The second wolf edged nearer, and Caleb hoofed him right behind the ear. It sounded like the crack of a baseball bat. The wolf twirled like a top, then crumpled. The first wolf stayed his distance as he snapped his jaws.

Crystal tried to steer Caleb back out into the water, but he was slow to take his eye off the wolves. Finally, he slid in for the ride back across the Flathead.

After a step or two into the water, both Crystal and Caleb relaxed when the wolves didn't follow. She saw Travis and Shawn headed their way. She waved at them to go on back.

She patted Caleb on the neck. "I owe you one. Boy, was I glad to see you!" She brought her feet up high in the saddle to keep them dry as they inched across the slick rocks and rapids.

"What happened back there?" she heard Shawn yell, as she made it to midstream.

"Wolves!" she yelled back with her hands cupped to her mouth. Just then Caleb slightly stumbled. She slid off on the downstream side and landed back first in the swift, frigid river.

For a second the water was so cold that Crystal couldn't get her breath. She fought to keep her head above water as she jostled over rocks down the river. She grabbed a series of panicked, short breaths.

Travis and Shawn were pushing their horses into the water after her, when all of a sudden, Teresa came splashing across the water riding the still-struggling Hawkeye. She threw the blanket from her shoulders to Crystal, holding tight to one end. "Grab it, Lil' Flash!" she shouted.

Crystal clutched it with all her might as Teresa, with her own legs hanging in the water, pulled her to shore. Gabrielle ran down with the other blanket and helped drag Crystal out of the water.

Travis retrieved Caleb from the river, and all of them clustered around Crystal. "We're all going to freeze to death for sure this time," Crystal said with teeth chattering. She noticed everyone was wet at least past their knees.

"Travis, did you bring any of those matches? We've got to dry out these clothes in a hurry." Shawn looked around. "Well, I'll be. Here comes the cavalry!"

The other four turned in time to see two snowmobiles charge down the hill toward the river. Soon, four others followed.

The first two snowmobiles were driven by members of the Kalispell search-and-rescue team. The other four contained Coach Duffy and several of the team members' fathers. Within a half hour the five wet riders changed to dry snowsuits that the rescuers brought and were headed back down the trail. Mr. Duffy brought in the horses.

It was 5:05 p.m. when they drove into the parking lot at Glacier Village. The whole team came out to cheer when they drove up. After hearty hugs and greetings all around, Crystal and Gabrielle walked with Dusty back to their room.

"So they're taking Teresa to the hospital?"

Dusty inquired. "She sure didn't look herself. Do you think she's going to be OK?"

"Sure, but they've got to give her a good checkup . . . especially to look for frostbite . . ."

Crystal interrupted Gabrielle. "Dusty, you would not believe this day! In fact, I can't believe we're still living in the same twenty-four hours. It's incredible."

"Well, you guys better call your folks. They've been calling about every half hour all day long! What a zoo around here since you guys left. I think the whole Camas Prairie has been raring to drive over here themselves."

Gabrielle had the first shot at the phone. Crystal listened to the conversation and watched a few tears trickle from Gabrielle's eyes as she reviewed the day's events.

Then Crystal called her dad.

"Daddy? It's Crystal. . . . Yeah, I'm OK. In the motel in Kalispell. . . . Everyone's fine. I mean, Teresa's getting a checkup, I think she's all right. I love you, too, Dad. We had to go after Teresa. We just had to do it. Caleb took care of me again. You ought to pay him for baby-sitting. I'll tell you all about it later. Tell Mom she can stop praying now.

"I guess we'll be coming home in the morning. I probably won't be on time for church. But we'll all go to the Christmas Eve candlelight Communion. It's going to be a great Christmas. But, if you don't mind, I think I'll just stay in by

152

the fire all day. Yeah, me, too. 'Bye.''

It took well over an hour for Gabrielle and Crystal to finish their showers, fix their hair, and dress.

"Teresa's mom stopped by," Dusty informed them. "Teresa is fine, but they want to keep her in the hospital overnight, in case anything develops. You know, like pneumonia."

A loud banging at the door followed the last words.

"Anybody want to go out for ice cream?"

Crystal swung open the door, "Shawn! Travis! You nerds! Gabrielle, grab my coat; let's go eat."

As Crystal stood at the doorway she said, "Hey, everybody, since Teresa has to stay at the hospital, why don't we go over there and cheer her up? It would be fun to . . . wait a minute. Why are you all looking at me like that?"

"Go cheer up Teresa? GO CHEER UP TERESA! That's what you said at five this morning. Remember?" Gabrielle almost shrieked.

"Look, I mean, I'm not talking about a big deal, just a . . ." Crystal noticed Gabrielle and Dusty sneaking up behind her with a pile of pillows.

"Hey, what's the big?"

Gabrielle tossed a pillow to Shawn and another to Travis. Now all four surrounded Crystal and started moving in. It reminded Crystal, just for a moment, of the scene with the wolves.

"Hey, wait a minute, you guys. Look, I just

said we should go cheer up Teresa. Now, if you don't want . . ."

At a signal from Shawn all four raised their pillows above their heads and advanced toward Crystal.

"This is not funny, you guys. This is definitely NOT . . ."

A wave of pillows crashed down on her head.

"Well, maybe," she laughed until she cried, "it's a little bit funny."

For adventure, excitement, and even romance . . .
Read these Quick Fox books

CRYSTAL Books by Stephen and Janet Bly

How many fourteen-year-old girls have been chased by the cavalry, stopped a stagecoach, tried rodeo riding, and discovered buried treasure? Crystal Blake has. You never know what new adventure Crystal will find in the next chapter!

1 Crystal's Perilous Ride
2 Crystal's Solid Gold Discovery
3 Crystal's Rodeo Debut
4 Crystal's Mill Town Mystery
5 Crystal's Blizzard Trek
6 Crystal's Grand Entry

MARCIA Books by Norma Jean Lutz

Marcia Stallings has every girl's dream—her own horse! And she intends to pursue her dream of following her mother's footsteps into the show arena—no matter what the obstacles.

1 Good-bye, Beedee
2 Once Over Lightly